DeAD WoRRieD!

MOYA SIMONS

DEAD !
WORRIED!

ORCHARD BOOKS

ORCHARD BOOKS
96 Leonard Street, London EC2A 4RH
Orchard Books Australia
14 Mars Road, Lane Cove, NSW 2066
ISBN 1 86039 255 5 (hardback)
ISBN 1 86039 312 8 (paperback)
First published in Great Britain 1996
First paperback publication 1996
A CIP catalogue record for this book is
available from the British Library.
Printed in Great Britain

Contents

For Tahli and Liora

Calm Down, Mr King

Mr King is my school teacher. He's OK, even if he gets a bit worked up some days. Today is one of those days. Behind his steaming glasses, his eyes are glazed with emotion.

"So, Year 6, if we are going to produce some good creative writing for you to take home to your suffering parents, we've got to have creative input. Do you know what input means, Corky?"

Corky, my best mate, blinks and says, "Input. Like output but different. Yes. Sure. Input. Let me think. Um. Putting something in. Yeah."

Mr King glares at him. "That was a lucky guess, Corky." He removes his glasses, wipes them, blots the damp patch on his forehead and breathes heavily.

"We all have to, as Corky so eloquently explained, 'put something in'. So today we are going to broaden our creative horizons. We are going to learn about similes. Does anyone know what similes are?"

The class fidgets. Taffy Douglas sits a couple of rows in front of me. He's a heavy guy with large shoulders and small eyes. Taffy's plucking hairs from the back of his head so there may be a nit bunjee-jumping around there. Mandy Miller, who makes me go hot and cold, is studying the cute tooth pattern at the end of her pencil. Her best friend, Gretta Licz, is having an out-of-body experience somewhere on the Barrier Reef.

Mr King says sadly, "I'll explain. Now, look out the window at the sky. See those little white clouds drifting by. Go on, look. Taffy Douglas, do as you're told and stop pulling at your hair."

"It's a nervous habit," says Taffy.

"I'm not interested in your nervous habits," says Mr King. "Just look out the window at the sky."

So we turn our heads and try to stay awake as we watch the clouds flutter by.

"Now," says Mr King. "A simile is when you compare one thing with another. You could say, for example, that the clouds are like tufts of cottonwool. Can someone give me another example?"

Taffy holds up his free hand and says, "The clouds are like bits of the white of an egg that got separated from the yolk."

Mr King strokes his chin. "Well, yes, Taffy, I'd have liked something a bit more poetic but that's the idea. Now, let's just look again at the sky. There's the sun over there. Birds streaking past. Any more similes from the class? Come on. Put your thinking caps on."

Mandy waves her hand. "The sky is like a sea of blue milk."

"A sea of blue milk? Have you ever seen blue milk? Still, at least you're thinking creatively."

I call out, "The sun looks like a runny egg yolk."

Taffy says, "Those dark clouds over there look like burnt toast."

"Hey," says Corky excitedly. "This is very cool. We've got a whole breakfast out there."

"Yes, well, it's a start anyway," says Mr King. "Now, for homework I want you to write ten sentences in which you use similes. The other thing I want to discuss with you is correct speech. It alarms and saddens me that a lot of you seem to communicate inappropriately. English is a rich language. Try to learn to express yourselves properly. Danny

Thompson, what are you doing?"

What I'm doing is going nuts. Taffy keeps pulling hairs out of the back of his head. I've just thrown my glow-in-the-dark eraser at his plucking hand.

"Huh," I say innocently to Mr King. "It's amazing. My eraser sort of, kind of, bounced off my hand. It moved through the air like a rocket ship. Hey, isn't that like, um, a simile, huh?"

Mr King's face turns purple.

"Danny Thompson. You corrupt English with your 'huhs' and 'sort ofs' and 'kind ofs', and you're a disruptive influence. You can stay in class at lunch-time and concentrate on similes."

I want to tell Mr King that he's over-reacting, that I'm really a good kid, but the bell goes for recess.

As we troop out the classroom I say to Corky, "What's with him? He's so moody today."

Corky says, "He's in a bad way. His wife's going to have a baby. My mum knows Mrs King, that's how I know. Mr King goes along with his wife to these birth classes and he's really involved. He's going to be with her when the baby is born and do all that stuff like holding her hand and telling her how to breathe. Then when the doctor says it's time to push the baby out, he encourages her. Yeah, I know, it's kind of gross. Anyway, the baby was due a week ago and it's obviously very comfortable floating around

4

inside Mrs King because it hasn't arrived. Mr King's going nuts."

Mr King was about to become a father. About to be the proud dad of a squealing, stinky, twitching, dribbling baby. Poor Mr King. He doesn't know that now is the easy part. He should encourage the baby to stay put. Not to come out into the world until it's toilet-trained. I am an expert at such things. Bub Tub, my baby sister (OK, Penny, if you insist on correct names) is like a leaking battleship. No matter how much water you bail out, she continues to leak and drop bombs.

When she's not doing that she's throwing up, drooling little slimy patterns down her chin, and screaming.

Taffy Douglas comes over to Corky and me at recess. He sits with us on the grass, holding an apple with one hand and plucking hair with the other.

"What's up?" I ask him. "Why are you pulling out your hair?"

"I'm nervous. It's my parents," says Taffy. "They're still in love and all that sloppy stuff, but they're talking about moving. I don't want to move. I want to stay here."

Not so long ago Taffy's parents were like two gangsters who'd taken out a contract on each other. Taffy was a wreck.

"You'll go bald if you don't stop," says Corky. "Have some bubblegum and forget about it."

"I can't forget about it."

"Can't you develop another nervous habit?" I suggest. "I sit two rows behind you, Taffy. It's making me nervous watching you pull out your hairs one by one. I may end up with my own nervous habit if you don't stop soon."

"Can't you pull the lobe of your ear instead when you stress out?" asks Corky. "Just give it a little tug. That way you get to keep your hair and Danny stays sane."

"I'll try," says Taffy.

After recess we enter the wonderful world of maths. Subtraction, multiplication and long division are very important if you are to manage your pocket money properly, so I try to concentrate.

In the middle of the lesson Mr King is called to the phone. He leaves the class in a hurry. He is sweating heavily.

"Bet that's his wife. Bet the baby is coming," says Corky.

I sit quietly and watch Mandy Miller. Light coming through the window settles on her hair. I think of similes.

Mandy's hair is like bright honey.

Mandy's little white teeth are like two rows of little

6

white Minties.

Mandy's nose is like a tiny hill with two caves at the bottom.

Mandy's smile is like an upside-down rainbow.

Watching her, I go hot and cold.

Paper planes dart around the room. Kids whistle. I study Mandy and day-dream. Taffy starts to pull out his hair again.

I throw a ruler at the back of his head just as Mr King walks into the room.

"Danny Thompson," he screams at me. "I can't leave this class for a moment without you getting up to mischief. What have you got to say for yourself?"

I can't think of a thing.

Mr King is clearly in a bad way. Obviously his wife isn't about to have the baby or he'd be out of here quicker than a space shuttle. It's not a good day for him. He removes his glasses continually and wipes them and I decide that if I can find out when his birthday is I'll buy him a de-mister. His handkerchief looks like one of Bub Tub's wet nappies. His neck is red and a large vein resembling a twisted tree stump is standing up in it.

Meanwhile I don't feel so good myself. I write Taffy a note.

"Dear Taffy, I will pay for your therapy. Please stop pulling out your hair. I may have to murder you

7

if you don't."

I pass this note to Corky who passes it to Gretta who passes it to Taffy. Taffy turns and nods nervously at me. He starts tugging his ear.

When the bell goes for lunch everyone gets up and leaves the classroom. Everyone, that is, except me.

I am grounded. Stuck like a magnet to my desk.

Mr King frowns at me.

"I want you to write sentences with similes in them, Danny Thompson. Put that vivid imagination of yours to good use. If you produce some decent work you can go off and have your lunch in half an hour."

I sigh, open my book, and chew on the end of my pen. Mr King, who is writing notes, glances at me.

"And try to get your speech patterns right, boy. Learn to express yourself clearly. The key to success in life is communication. Remember that."

"Yes, Mr King."

Outside I can hear kids having fun. Eating, chucking a ball around, while I sit waiting for inspiration. Suddenly light floods my brain.

I start to write.

The stars were like splotches of pigeon droppings.
His head was as bald as my sister's bottom.

I stare at nothing in particular, waiting for more light. A woman waddles into the classroom. It has to

8

be Mrs King because she is very pregnant. She holds one hand against her back and says to Mr King, "I thought I'd pop in and see you, dear. I didn't want to wait in the staffroom. It's so stuffy there."

Mr King looks alarmed. He jumps off his chair as if there are upright nails in it.

"Are you all right, darling. Is it … is it … time?"

"No, silly," says Mrs King. Mr King has a big crease on his forehead. He takes Mrs King's arm and helps her slide into his chair.

I quickly write down, "His forehead looked like an unironed shirt," then I stare at Mr and Mrs King while I wait for more ideas to come.

"I just couldn't sit still at home," says Mrs King. "I'm on my way to the doctor for another checkup. Phew, it's hot."

"Can I get you a cool drink?" Mr King leans over his wife, holding her hand.

"You know what I'd like more than anything else in the world?" says Mrs King.

"No, dear."

"Ginger beer. A large bottle of ginger beer. It would cool me down."

"I could slip out and buy some," says Mr King. Then he sees me staring at them. "Danny Thompson, leave your work on the desk. You can finish it tomorrow."

Mrs King smiles at me. She fans herself with one hand. "Let him stay. He can keep me company while you're gone. After all, we might have a boy like him one day."

Mr King turns pale at such a thought.

"I could send Danny for the ginger beer but he's capable of coming back with a jar of mustard. No, I'll go myself."

He darts out of the classroom.

Mrs King grabs Mr King's notes and fans herself.

"I wish this baby would come. Do you have any baby sisters or brothers, Danny?"

"Yes. I have a sister. She's still in nappies."

"Is she lots of fun?"

"Um, well …" I decide not to tell the truth. "Sure. Mum says babies are no work at all and they keep you young and happy."

Mrs King beams at me. She looks like a contented watermelon.

I bend my head and quickly add that to my list of similes.

She smiled like a contented watermelon.

"Ah. Oh," says Mrs King.

"Yes," I say politely, continuing to write. I am on a roll now.

He ran as quickly as a car without brakes, I write, thinking of Mr King dashing to the shop.

"Ah. Oh," says Mrs King.

"Yes," I say again, and then I look up curiously. Mrs King is holding onto her huge tummy, and her face is like a bowl of sour milk. Another simile. I quickly add it to my list.

"Ah, oh," says Mrs King.

It then occurs to me that Mrs King doesn't look too well.

"Are you OK, Mrs King? I mean, you know, you're not about to, um. No, that's not possible. Is it?"

My powers of communication must be better than I think because Mrs King understands exactly what I mean.

"The baby. It's coming. This is it. Oh my goodness!"

I sit glued to my chair.

"Help me," squeals Mrs King. "Oh, it's on its way."

I unstick myself from my seat and walk gingerly up to Mrs King. She really is a funny colour.

"Tell you what. I'll run down to the office and get someone to call an ambulance. Don't you worry about a thing. I've never heard of a baby being born in a classroom. Never. It couldn't happen. That's why I've never heard of it. You tell the baby to hang on."

As I try to pass her she grabs me by one arm. Pregnant women must be extra strong because I can't pull myself away.

"Don't leave me. I don't want to be alone. My husband will only be a moment. Ah. Oh."

When Mr King arrives about five minutes later, Mrs King is lying on the floor. She insists she is more comfortable there. I've made a pillow for her head from Mr King's papers.

Mr King take one look at his wife and nearly passes out. He shakes like a palm tree caught in a cyclone as he kneels down beside her.

"Hey, Mr King," I say. "Maybe now's the time you can use all that stuff you learnt at those birth classes."

"Uh … oh," says Mrs King.

Mr King is looking as worried as an astronaut on the wrong planet. "What classes?" he says. I can hardly see his eyes through the fine mist on his glasses. He is obviously in deep shock.

"You'd better call the ambulance, Mr King," I tell him. "She didn't want me to leave her. Don't worry. It's just the baby coming. Isn't it wonderful? Like a miracle. Is that a simile?"

Mr King doesn't hear me, which is probably just as well. Reality has suddenly hit him. He stares at his wife.

"Whatever you do, don't push," he says, then he jumps up, drops the ginger beer, and runs out of the classroom yelling, "My wife's having a father! I'm going to be a baby!"

Even though his communication is not all it should be, everyone understands exactly what he means.

Mr King goes off to the hospital with Mrs King. A relief teacher turns up to take our class. Taffy manages to drive him nuts in just two hours by continually tugging at his left ear.

Just before school finishes the headmaster comes into our class and tells us that Mrs King has given birth to a boy.

I guess it's too much to hope they'll call him Danny.

Baby
Talk

"Uggle da doody. Ga do ba dood. Ayo, Anny."

Bub Tub has woken me up. This is very sad as I'd just been dreaming I'd discovered a new galaxy full of aliens who looked like Mandy Miller.

Bub Tub puts her fat hand on my cheek.

"Ayo, Anny," she says again, while I wipe sleep from my eyes.

"G'day, Bub Tub. You stink."

"Ga boom," says Bub Tub, which as everyone knows means, "So what." She toddles away.

I struggle out of bed and into the kitchen. It's a

warm Saturday morning. Dad is sitting at the breakfast table talking to Mum.

"I don't know, Madeline. I don't like the sound of it."

"Roger, it's a fun way to raise money for the farmers. It's all for a good cause."

"What is?" I say.

"Ba boom," says Bub Tub as she plonks herself on the floor and looks for dust to nibble.

"It's fine that it's for charity, but why can't they have a concert or a fete?"

"I don't know, Roger. This is what they came up with and everyone thought it was a good idea. It's a nice community project and it'll be fun."

"What will be?" I ask.

"Da doom," says Bub Tub.

"Everyone entering pays twenty dollars. They've already got nearly a hundred children. That's two thousand dollars, Roger."

"You're not selling me, are you?" I ask as I butter toast.

Mum looks at me. "Oh, no, Danny. Not that you wouldn't fetch a decent price."

Dad scratches his chin. "There's a thought."

"So, what's happening?" I ask as I stuff toast in my mouth.

"There's going to be a cute baby competition. It's

to raise money for the farmers—to help them over the drought."

"A cute baby competition? How can babies be cute? You're not thinking of entering Bub Tub?"

"Babies are very cute," says Mum stiffly. "And of course we're entering Bub Tub, aren't we, Roger?"

Mum's eyes are like two steel knobs as she focuses on my father. Dad gets up from the kitchen table and says hastily, "Oh well, OK, if it means so much to you. I just don't like the idea of my little girl being in a beauty contest. It's one big meat market."

"Oh, Roger. She's not even two. Don't be silly."

"Hey, does Bub Tub get to toddle down a catwalk in a bikini?"

"You stop being silly, too, Danny. She'll just sit there along with a lot of other babies and some judge will pick out the most appealing baby. First prize is a medal."

"Is it made of chocolate?"

"You two," says Mum, shaking her head.

Dad kisses Mum goodbye, bends down and picks dust out of Bub Tub's hand and then ruffles my hair. He's on his way to work at his delicatessen where he sells smelly cheese, salami, toilet paper and tomato soup.

"I'll see you all later."

After breakfast I sit down on the kitchen floor

with Bub Tub.

"Ook, Anny," she squeals. In her hand she has two small curls of dusty fluff, a twitching fly and a legless beetle.

She mixes the dust with the insects and starts to put this tasty sandwich into her mouth.

"Hold on, Bub Tub. You'll get sick." I pry the mangled insects and dust from her fat hands. She screams.

Later, while Bub Tub bangs a few saucepans together, I help Mum pile plates in the sink.

"Are you really going to enter Bub Tub in a cute baby competition? I mean, I know you think she's cute, but if she does a poo when the judges are looking at her they could end up in hospital from the smell."

Mum says crossly, "Don't carry on. Bubby's nearly toilet-trained."

Nearly toilet-trained. What my mum means is that Bub Tub has been trained to *nearly* reach her potty before she does it in her nappy.

Mum tells me that the competition is the following Sunday. She expects me to be there.

"You're to come, and that's that. We're going as a family. Stop pulling that face, Danny. There'll be other children you know there. I met the mother of that girl in your class, what's her name, Mandy Miller, at the canteen last week. Mandy's going along to support her young cousin, Brett."

"Mandy?"

I turn my face away and start to count the magnets on the fridge. That's so Mum won't notice that I've gone sweaty.

The week comes and goes. Corky gets into trouble for putting a grasshopper in Gretta's lunchbag. Taffy reckons that since he started to pull his left ear lobe when he's nervous it is now a centimetre longer than the right one. Mandy discusses the forthcoming baby contest.

"My cousin Brett is about twenty months old. He talks this cute baby talk."

"He should get on very well with Bub Tub," I tell her.

My eyes fog over as I imagine the scene.

"Ga doom. Da gigle ba boom," says Baby Brett as he heads a conference for global peace.

"Da doody ba phllub," replies Bub Tub, thumping her fat fist on a long desk.

They are surrounded by reporters who are dazzled by their verbal skills. The next day this headline appears: "Bub Tub and Brett, the wonder babies, outline amazing plan for world peace."

"Hey, Danny, you aren't listening to me." Mandy

flicks her soft little fingers in front of my eyes.

"Huh?"

Sunday comes. Bub Tub is wearing a lemon-coloured dress. The lemon is approximately the same colour as her vomit so we are hoping that if she throws up no one will notice. Mum has put a tiny yellow ribbon in the scrap of fair hair that Bub Tub has growing on the top of her head.

Dad carefully wipes dribble off Bub Tub's permanently moist chin. He checks Bub Tub's nappy. "That's a good girl," he says. "Nice and dry."

"You're talking about the weather," I say to him as I check that I've got a decent supply of bubblegum in my pocket. "Bub Tub's nappy is never nice and dry."

We drive to Bayview Park, which has lots of grass and is fringed with shady trees. Next to it is a large expanse of blue water. There are small craft on the water, and a public swimming pool next to the pier. Frankly, I'd rather be swimming than attending a dumb cute baby contest, but there is nothing I can do. My parents insist on family togetherness.

Right now Bayview Park is filled with people and babies. There are tables everywhere covered with bright cloths, and happy people are selling everything from sausage sandwiches to fairy floss. The cute baby contest is to start at three o'clock.

It is a very off thing to be here with my family, but then again the sausage sandwiches look good and isn't that Mandy Miller over there standing near a tree?

It is, and she is wearing shorts and a T-shirt. Her legs are pink and she's wearing a big sun hat, which is a shame because the sun doesn't get to light up her hair and make it shiny.

While Mum and Dad go and check that Bub Tub is registered as an entrant for the contest, I wander over to Mandy.

"Where's your cousin Brett?"

Mandy points to a pale-looking kid sitting on a big tartan blanket. He has a sunsuit on and a bib around his neck. His lower lip is jerking as if it's trying to find a way to escape from his jaw.

"He's been crying. It's hot and he's bored. Where's your little sister?"

So I take Mandy with me to look for Mum and Dad. While we do that I shout her some bubblegum and she shares half of a sausage sandwich with me.

Mum and Dad have put a picnic basket on a large blanket. Dad is waving flies away from Bub Tub's face and Bub Tub is trying to catch them.

"Your baby sister—she's so, so …"

Mandy can't find the right word to say how cute she thinks Bub Tub is. Mandy definitely doesn't understand what cuteness is.

She wanders back to her family and comes back after a while carrying Brett.

Mum goes soppy and gives Brett, who looks like he's discovered he is one number short in Lotto, a big hug. Bub Tub squeals, so Mandy gives her a big hug. We sit the babies next to one another on the blanket. They ignore each other at first, then Bub Tub reaches out her chubby fingers and touches Brett on his cheek.

"Ayo."

This profound statement is followed by more profound statements as Brett and Bub Tub discover each other.

"Phlumb."

"Iggle bug."

"Da doody."

The two of them sit there chomping on grass and beetles while Mum and Dad nick off to buy some drinks.

They return a few minutes later and we sit there eating sausage sandwiches and drinking strawberry soda. The sun is warm. Bub Tub and Brett begin to whinge and fidget. Bub Tub pulls Brett's hair. He's only got a few bits of fuzz on the top of his head so I reckon she's got very keen eyesight.

Brett squeals, "Ga bod. Iffle flug." He tugs at Bub Tub's bib.

"Now stop it you two," says Mum. Just when it looks like we're going to have to send them to opposite sides of a boxing ring, some guy holding a big loudspeaker says, "The judging is about to commence. Will you bring your babies over here. Form a line and we'll get on with the show!"

Brett's parents appear quicker than ants at a picnic.

They wipe his face and brush his little bit of fuzz. Mum takes a tissue from her bag and wipes the last trickle of dribble from Bub Tub's chin. The heat is on. Mandy says to me, "Good luck with Bub Tub."

Then she gets up and goes with her aunt and uncle to the judging area. Mum straightens Bub Tub's yellow bow. Bub Tub squirms and wriggles. Then she focuses her little eyes on me.

"Ayo, Anny."

I go cross-eyed. She smiles.

"Now just keep smiling like that for the judges, Muffin," says Dad.

We take Bub Tub over to a grassy area free from bits of dropped sausage and chips. Three people are sitting in front of a large wooden table. Next to them stands a tall man holding a microphone.

As anxious mums or dads scramble forward holding their squirming kids, Dad and I stand back with all the other relatives and friends.

"Go, Bub Tub. Go!" I say to Bub Tub as Mum

carries her away to the judging area.

"Ta ta, Anny," says Bub Tub. She waves her fat fingers at me.

I look at all these off kids being held by their parents. What a weird bunch!

One kid is wearing a blue sunsuit. He has about fourteen chins and a stomach like a balloon. He could pass for a midget sumo wrestler. Then there's a baby with yellow spiky hair, chomping on a dummy. She looks just like Maggie from "The Simpsons". That one there resembles a little bald old man. And the little kid near Bub Tub looks a bit like a basset hound.

There are skinny babies and fat ones. Ones with toothless smiles and others that can't stop crying.

Brett's mum stands beside my mum. The judges slowly move around the long line of parents and babies.

"Our esteemed judges today," says the guy with the mike, "are Percy Preston, local photographer, Diana Thorne, from the magazine *Mother and Child*, and Bronwyn Fillip from the *Herald*."

Everybody claps politely.

The judges take out notebooks and peer at the babies. They write things down which I guess are cuteness ratings.

The judge from the *Herald* gets carried away with

all the cuteness.

"What a dear little coochy-coo," she says to one baby who immediately starts to cry.

"Who's a little cutie pie?" she asks another kid who promptly blows a raspberry at her.

Then she comes to Brett.

"Now here's a dimple-dumpling face."

"Phlub," says Brett.

The judge giggles. Brett's mother giggles. Brett begins to turn from pink to red. I know what that means. He's filling his nappy. His mum knows it too. She's holding him in her arms with one hand supporting his bum. The smile on her face turns crooked as she struggles to look thrilled.

"What lovely red cheeks he has," says the judge.

I've got to admit that a full nappy does wonders for Brett's complexion. He's straining and his cheeks are the colour of ripe tomatoes as last night's mashed banana passes right through him.

The judge writes something in her cuteness rating book and then comes to Bub Tub. A small insect has settled on the end of Bub Tub's nose. Bub Tub is fascinated.

"Another little uddledums," says the judge. Bub Tub begins to drool. It's the insect at the end of her nose. It's looking very tasty, and I can tell she's thinking up ways to encourage it to roll down her nose to her mouth where her little pink tongue is poised ready to catch it.

Somehow, Brett and Bub Tub make it through the first round. Mortified parents, who have to cope with the fact that their kids are low in the cuteness stakes, leave the judging area.

Mum comes running over to us with Bub Tub. She's as excited as a flea on a dog's back. "We've made it to the semi-finals!"

Dad nods happily and pats Bub Tub on her cheek. Mandy dashes over to me. "Isn't it great? Both our babies are still in the contest." She doesn't have her sun hat on and her hair is speckled with light.

Ten babies, most of whom are beginning to feel hot and tired, are in the semi-finals. One kid can't take it any more. He gives a bloodcurdling scream and his dad has to withdraw him from the contest. Good. That just leaves nine.

The judges go from baby to baby again. The photographer, Percy Preston, stares thoughtfully at Brett. Brett, who has had a nappy change and is now looking rather pale, begins to sneeze. Two green globs of yuk become attached to the bottom of both nostrils. His mum tries to wipe his nose quickly but more yuk forms. The photographer shudders and writes something down in his notebook, then moves on to Bub Tub.

Bub Tub, who is waving a chubby hand at the air trying to catch more insects, sees the photographer and gives him a very cute smile. He is charmed. He smiles back.

He writes in his notebook. Dad nudges me. We both know that he's been bowled over by Bub Tub's cuteness.

The photographer reaches over to pat Bub Tub's cheek. Bad mistake. She grabs his outstretched fingers and puts his pinkie in her mouth.

Bub Tub, who has cut her teeth on rusks, hard pieces of toast and snail shells, has teeth like razor blades. She bites.

The photographer screams. He struggles hard to free his pinkie, then says a number of unfair and rude words about my sister.

He wipes his mutilated finger. Then he crosses something out in his notebook.

Brett and Bub Tub do not make it to the finals. Three smiling little kids do. They do not scowl, scream, sneeze or go cross-eyed. They do not bite judges. They just sit there placidly, gurgling away.

The winner is the kid who looks like a sumo wrestler.

Everybody claps politely. The cameras flash just as the kid throws up.

Later Mandy and I sit down on the grass eating

chips while Bub Tub and Brett play together.

"I reckon the judges are nuts," says Mandy. "Our babies have real class."

I look at Bub Tub and Brett. They are having a competition to see who can produce the most dribble.

Bub Tub and Brett are like two leaking dams.

"You're dead right Mandy," I say. "They've got real class."

A Bet with Helen the Horrible

"Want to come to the pictures with me on Saturday? *The Alien Nerd* is on."

Corky and I have just jumped the school fence after school. Corky hands me some mint-flavoured bubblegum and we walk along Mulberry Lane blowing pale spidery bubbles.

"*The Alien Nerd*? Sounds like the life story of my sister," says Corky. "Yeah, I'll come. I'm dead lucky I've got enough money left to go anywhere."

"Why? What happened?"

So Corky tells me this story about his sister, Helen the Horrible:

Helen is always talking. She's like a wound-up Barbie doll. She hardly stops to breathe. It's amazing. She should be written up in a book about scientific mysteries. The only time she stops is when she's eating or sleeping.

Last Sunday afternoon, my parents were out. All I wanted to do was swim a few laps of the pool in peace. I didn't want her gabbing around the place with her whining voice. You wouldn't understand, Danny. Bub Tub may stink, but she just babbles away in baby talk. And when she's munching on beetles and snails, she doesn't talk at all.

Helen's a maniac. She was going on and on. "She said, he said, they did, we went." It was giving me a king-size headache.

She hung around the pool like a bad smell. The sports carnival's on soon and I wanted to improve my swimming. I wanted Helen to go far away. I had the Simpson Desert in mind but even the front garden would have helped.

I said to her, "Shut up, Helen the Horrible."

She said to me, "You slimy weasel. You fossilised frog." She went on and on. I tried swimming underwater but she put on her cozzie and jumped in the pool. She appeared underwater blowing bubbles and making rude signs with her finger.

Finally, I couldn't stand her any more.

My sister loves talking and boys more than anything, but money runs a close third. "Helen," I said, "I bet you twenty dollars, all the money I have in the world, that you can't shut up for two hours."

Helen's mean little eyes gleamed like polished marbles. Her mean little mouth twisted into an almost human smile.

"Are you serious, vomit face?"

I knew what I was doing. There was no way in the world that Helen could stop talking for two hours.

"This is cool," she said to me. "Easy money." She smiled again. Her pointy eye teeth slid over her lower lip and she looked exactly like a vampire.

I climbed out of the pool, and we sat there working out some rules.

1. She had to shut up, yet be where I could check on her.

2. She couldn't pull faces at me or make rude signs with her fingers.

3. She couldn't write notes.

4. The bet was to begin at 2.30 and stop at 4.30. After 4.30 if Helen had not spoken I was to immediately pay her twenty dollars. If she spoke before 4.30

she had to pay me twenty dollars.

"This is the easiest money I'm ever going to make," said Helen.

It was then a quarter past two. For fifteen minutes Helen talked non-stop. It was as if she had to get rid of every word that had ever formed in her brain in preparation for the long drought. I put cottonwool in my ears as I sat by the pool. Helen jumped in front of me, she jumped around me. She leapt into the pool. She swam a few laps. All the time her mouth was opening and closing like a pair of garden shears: "He said, they said, she did, he went, they went."

I kept my eyes on my watch. I was hoping she'd go past 2.30 and then I'd be an outright winner. However, just before half past two Helen glanced at her waterproof watch, and the world suddenly turned silent. All I could hear was the swish of water as Helen swam. It was a miracle. She'd shut up.

Well, it was my turn then. I leapt into the water. I tickled her ribs. I sat on her head. Did my sister scream at me? No, though her fang-like teeth shot out and her eyes were like two cannonballs. If looks could kill I'd be in heaven right now, but she didn't say a word.

I swam a few lengths while Helen got out of the pool and dried herself. She gave me a sick, mysterious smile, then sprawled out on a towel, smothered herself with suncream and promptly shut her eyes.

"Hey," I called out. "That's not fair. You're supposed to stay awake."

But you see, we hadn't said anything about staying awake in the rules. I started to get worried. When Helen falls asleep it's as if an elephant's jumped on her head. Nothing wakes her. I couldn't afford to lose twenty dollars. It had taken me ages to save it.

I stood beside her and began to drip water on her. She didn't budge. She just breathed deeply and curled up on her side.

I screamed at her, "Has anyone told you lately that you look like a bunged-up toilet? Your nose is so long it might join up with your mouth, then you'll have to breathe through your ears when you eat. If you get any more zits your face will have more craters than the moon. Do you know you're growing heaps of hair on your legs? You look like an ape woman."

I followed this with ape noises. I even grabbed a banana from the kitchen and threw it at her. It landed on her head. She just continued to lie there with this sick smile on her face, her eyes tightly closed.

Twenty dollars! I could see my money disappearing before my eyes. What could I do?

Then it came to me. John the Jerk. He's a guy that Helen likes. She makes gaga eyes at him when she sees him. And he's got some serious brain problem because he likes her. He tells her she's cute. Helen. The one who makes Dracula seem good-looking.

I went inside the house. This was risky, because Helen was probably muttering to herself at top speed in the garden and I'd never know.

I ran to Helen's bedroom. I found her little red book. The one with all the phone numbers of her daggy friends. I phoned John the Jerk. I offered him ten dollars if he could get Helen to speak.

"Easy," he said. "Just tell her I'm on the phone. Tell her I want to ask her out. But don't you go back on our deal. I'll be over later to get my money."

"Yeah, sure," I muttered. What a world we live in. No one will do anything for nothing.

I ran out to the garden. Helen was sprawled on her towel like a large two-legged spider. Her mouth was buried in the towel and although I couldn't prove it, I'm sure she was talking to herself.

"Hey, Helen," I called out. "John the Jerk's on the phone. He said to ask you if he can take you out. I told him I'd speak to you about it but I didn't think you could come to the phone. I said you're not going to be able to talk until after 4.30. He didn't seem real impressed. He seemed to want an answer now. Maybe I should tell him to ask someone else out—what do you reckon?"

My sister jumped up as if she'd been stung by a

bee. She punched the air. Her face turned tomato-sauce red. She screwed up her face. Her eyes began to roll backwards into her head. I thought she'd been possessed, like that girl we saw in a movie who got taken over by a devil.

Suddenly from Helen's mouth came this blood-curdling scream.

"You rotten slimy toad," she said. "You demented snail. I'll get you one day."

She took off. She ran into the house like she was training for the Year 2000 Olympics.

I ran after her. This was a lot of fun. She picked up the phone, took a deep breath, and in her Saint Helen voice said, "Hi John."

They talked and carried on for a while. I left the kitchen. It was getting boring. All I wanted now was Helen's twenty dollars. Even if I had to give ten dollars to John the Jerk I'd still be ahead.

I was just planning what I'd spend my money on when Helen came up to me.

"Have to give you the money you won another time, toad. John's taking me bowling. He said he's come into some money. But he only has enough for his own games. I'll need my own money. He'll be around soon."

And with that my sister, who'd always told me that a bet was a bet, went back on our deal. She disappeared inside the bathroom and I knew that it'd be easier to get a vampire to change its diet than to get my sister to pay up.

Later, John the Jerk came over. Helen was still in the bathroom, probably trying to file her pointed teeth. He grabbed me by the sleeve and said, "I want my money and I want it now."

I noticed that he had a few pointed teeth as well, so I decided to pay up. That left me with ten dollars when I should have had thirty. I was starting to feel pretty miserable. But then I got an idea.

"John," I said. "I bet you the last ten dollars I have in the world that you'll kiss Helen within one hour."

John the Jerk looked at me and shook his head. "I hate taking money from a kid, but you're on. I could do with the extra cash."

While John flicked through some of my comics I caught up with Helen as she came out of the bathroom smelling like dead flowers.

"Helen," I said, "I'm only telling you this because I don't want bad feelings between us. John told me he's crazy about you. He can hardly stop himself from putting his arms around you. He's dying to kiss you but he's afraid you'll go cold on him."

Helen should have been suspicious, but she wasn't because I'd told her something she was dying to hear. Her beady eyes lit up like traffic lights.

"John? Kiss? Arms?" Her voice was thick with excitement.

I walked behind her as she went into my bedroom. John was sitting on my bed reading a Superman comic.

She sat down next to John. She quietly moved the comic away. She gave him her best Saint Helen look. He said, "Huh?"

"It's OK, John. I get shy sometimes too," said my sister as she moved in for the kill.

John sat there like a packet of frozen peas. Helen shut her eyes, and with the accuracy of a test cricketer landed a beaut kiss on John's stunned lips. He tried to push her away. One of his eyes rolled around in its socket as he looked at me.

I knew what he was thinking, but he didn't know my sister. This was her moment in time. This was what she'd been living her life for.

John, who is sixteen and likes girls a lot, tried to push Helen away, but failed. He gave in to the passion of the moment. Helen coming on to him was more than he could stand.

While they stayed locked in a sweaty kiss, I nicked over to John. I took my ten dollars from his top pocket.

They never did get to go bowling. Mum and Dad came home just when Helen the Horrible and John the Jerk were setting a world record for the longest kiss.

They hadn't heard a thing. Dad walked into my bedroom while I was sitting on the carpet reading. Helen and John were still at it. Slobbering over each other.

Dad made this kind of funny noise. Something between a dog's howl and a cat's hiss. Anyway, they stopped kissing quick smart, and as far as I know John the Jerk was last seen running in the direction of Melbourne with my dad trying to catch him.

"Wow, that's some story, Corky," I tell him. "But you know it's just not fair that Helen got out of paying you. A bet's a bet."

"That doesn't worry me one bit," says Corky. "Helen's got laryngitis. She reckons she caught a bug, but I reckon her voice was so over-worked it just went on strike. She can't say a word. She walks around the house holding up signs when she has to talk."

"Hey, that's great news."

"It's the best," says Corky. "My house is so happy and quiet. Just like a cemetery."

We explode a few more bubbles and head for home.

Seeing **T**hings **C**learly

There's something up with Mandy Miller. She's always been super smart at school. When Mr King asks a question her hand shoots up like a rocket. Mr King once said, "Mandy, it is children like you who make my job as a teacher a pleasure."

That's how I know there's something wrong. She's become really quiet in class. There's a wriggly frown between her eyes, and the corners of her mouth droop like two sad commas.

The other day Mr King said to her, "Mandy, read out what I've written on the blackboard."

Mandy screwed up her eyes, stared at the blackboard, looked at Mr King and then at her shoes. "I've got a sore throat," she said. Then she gave a gigantic cough. Mr King jumped in surprise.

"That's a huge cough, but it shouldn't stop you reading from the blackboard."

Mandy put both her hands to her throat. "Can't talk," she said, and her voice sounded like it was stuck at the bottom of a deep well. Mr King frowned and peered at the rest of us.

"Taffy, read what's on the blackboard, and please leave the lobe of your ear alone."

Taffy stopped tugging his ear and read, "What is a metaphor?"

Now I watch Mandy as she fiddles with her pen during class. Her face is sad.

At recess she sits with her best friend Gretta Licz, talking quietly. I wander over to her.

"G'day, how's things?" I ask casually.

Mandy glances at me, then away. "OK. Not bad. Awful."

"Huh? What's up?"

"I don't want to talk about it," says Mandy and she presses her mouth tightly into a hard line.

"Go away, Danny, or I'll whack you. Can't you see Mandy doesn't want you around?" says Gretta, and she gives me a dirty look.

"No, let him stay," says Mandy. She finishes the apricot she's eating, puts the stone neatly in a brown paper bag, then squints up at me.

"Maybe you can tell me what you think about it?"

"Think about what?" I squat down beside them.

"I've got to wear glasses," says Mandy. Absently, she starts to pull out bits of grass.

"Glasses? Is that all?" I try to imagine Mandy's eyes framed by glasses. "Is that so bad?"

"It's terrible," she says. She fumbles with the paper bag. "Everyone will tease me."

"I won't tease you," I say quickly. "Glasses aren't so awful. It could be worse."

"I can't think of anything worse," says Mandy.

"Yes, I agree," Gretta butts in. She pats Mandy on her back. "There's nothing worse, except maybe a face full of zits. Anyway, if anyone teases you, I'll whack them, that's what I'll do."

"When are you getting your glasses?" I ask Mandy.

"This afternoon after school. Mum's taking me to the optician's to pick them up."

"When did your vision, um go?" I ask politely.

"A few weeks ago I woke up and thought I had sleep stuck in my eyes. Everything was blurred. I kept washing my eyes, but I still couldn't see properly. I think it's got worse since then. I can hardly make out the words on the blackboard. I'm too embarrassed to tell Mr King because he'll make me sit at the front until I get my glasses. It's awful. When I wear them everyone will stare at me."

"If they do I'll whack them," says Gretta.

The bell goes. Mandy stands up. Gretta takes her arm. Mandy pushes her away.

"Quit it, Gretta. I *can* see, you know. I'm just short-sighted. Stop making things worse. And Danny, stop staring at me, and don't make fun of me when I get my glasses."

"I'll whack you if you do," says Gretta.

What do they take me for? Still, as I walk away I think about Mandy's eyes being hidden by glasses. I think of the way her little nose will be made smaller by glasses perched on it. I think of how everyone teased Evelyn Burnie when she came to school one day wearing a pair of glasses. She was smiling and saying how good it was to see us because she'd never seen us properly before.

"Hey, Evelyn, did you grow an extra pair of eyes last night?" Taffy asked her.

"What's life like living behind two glass windows?" I said. It was pretty rotten of us and I never thought twice about Evelyn Burnie's sad face as she turned away. Next term she went to another school and I hope the kids were kinder to her there.

Mandy wearing glasses? Could it be some mistake?

41

I watch her during the afternoon. While we are all writing down colourful sentences, she's squinting at the blackboard. I guess she really does need them.

When I leave school in the afternoon I tell Corky about Mandy.

"Glasses," says Corky. "Mandy wearing glasses. Poor kid."

"Don't you think you're carrying on a bit? It's not like she's going to die. They're just glasses. She could have a face covered with zits."

"Maybe she'll get those too. Zits and glasses. Phew!"

After dinner that night we sit in front of the TV. We're watching "The Simpsons". Bub Tub is standing on my foot blowing dribble-bubbles at me. Mum's writing a letter and Dad is glued to the TV saying things like, "That Homer Simpson. That Bart. They're too much for me."

He's clapping one hand against his knee as he laughs. Dad's wearing glasses. Funny how I've never thought about it before. Gold-rimmed glasses. I can't remember noticing them for ages. It's like they've become part of his face.

"How long have you worn glasses?" I ask him.

"Ha ha, that Bart Simpson. He's so revolting it's hilarious. What's that you said? Glasses? I've had this pair for about five years. Ha ha, look at them go!"

"Hey, Mum," I say. "Did you have to wear glasses when you were at school?"

Mum pauses in her letter writing. She sucks the end of her pen and thinks.

"Now you come to mention it, I did. I wore them for about three years from when I was nine until I turned twelve. I hated wearing them at first, but then I got used to them."

I try to imagine Mum sitting in class hiding behind her glasses. Bub Tub interrupts my thoughts by biting my leg.

"Go away, Bub Tub. Find some nice little beetle to eat."

"Uggle da doody," says Bub Tub and she wanders off. Imagine if Bub Tub had to wear glasses. She'd look pretty clever. Like a baby professor. Then I wonder about that. Wearing glasses doesn't mean you're clever. You could be stupid and wear glasses. So why does everyone think that wearing them makes you a geek?

The next day Mandy arrives at school wearing her new glasses. They are small with pale pink frames. I don't know why she made such a fuss. She looks as if she's got little pink shells around her blue eyes, otherwise she's just the same. The sun still makes her hair go shiny, and I still go hot and cold when I see her.

I run over to her as she stands near the canteen with Gretta. "Hi, Mandy. Um, your glasses are OK."

She pulls a face at me. "What's that supposed to mean? Why are you being nice to me? Why did you mention my glasses?"

"I'm going to whack you, Danny Thompson," says Gretta. "Honestly, you are so insensitive."

I walk away. Girls. I will never understand them. I run into Taffy Douglas. He's still tugging his ear lobe.

"How's things, Taffy? Do your parents still want to move?"

"I wouldn't be pulling my ear lobe if they'd decided to stay. That's a pretty stupid question."

I just don't seem able to say the right thing today. Kids start to tease Mandy as soon as they see her.

"Well, look who's turned into the class geek."

"Now you've got four eyes does that mean you see two of everything?"

I want to jump in front of Mandy and protect her. I want to punch all those rotten kids who call her names, but I don't. I just hang around with my hands in my pockets and do nothing. Corky doesn't call Mandy names, which is just as well, as I don't know how I'd handle it. Taffy is so busy pulling his ear lobe he doesn't notice anything different about her.

44

Gretta tries to protect Mandy. "I'll whack you," she says to anyone who passes a nasty remark. She flashes her beady little eyes and waves her hands around and tries to look threatening.

Mr King, king of the bright sparks, says to Mandy in class, "Well, now I understand why you've been so inattentive lately. You needed glasses. And they look very nice on you. Very nice." He pushes his own up the bridge of his nose, which I guess is his way of showing support, while Gretta says softly, "I'm going to whack him if he doesn't shut up."

Mandy is very quiet in class. She doesn't answer any questions. She stares at her workbook with a mournful expression on her face.

Finally, I can't stand it. I write her a note. "Cheer up. By tomorrow no one will notice your glasses."

I send it to her via Taffy who passes it to Gretta who sits next to Mandy. This is a big mistake. Gretta reads it, glares at me, tears it up, and writes me a note. Taffy passes it to me. It says, "I'm going to whack you, Danny Thompson. Signed Gretta Licz."

The day draws to an end. The kids who teased Mandy at the beginning of the day are now bored with her glasses. As for me, the more I see Mandy with her glasses, the hotter and colder I get. They just do something to me—those bright blue eyes circled by those pink seashell frames.

Gretta finally unsticks herself from Mandy at the school gates. She has to catch a bus home. Corky is on his way to the dentist so I start to walk home alone.

"Hey." I turn around. It's Mandy. She catches up with me. She stares at me, then looks at the pavement. "I know you wanted to say nice things to me, but nothing helps. I'll never get used to glasses. I hate them so much. I feel so ugly."

"*Ugly*?" I turn to her. "*You* feel *ugly*? That's nuts."

I stop at the newsagency. "Come in with me for a sec. I'm buying a Lance Spear comic."

Mandy shrugs her shoulders. "I'd better get home."

She give me this sad smile, then swings her bag and walks away.

The next day everyone's forgotten about Mandy's glasses. Someone has put a dye in the boys' toilets and the water is flushing bright purple, which was a shock for me as I thought my pee had changed colour.

Mrs King brings in her new baby to show the class. I can't understand why everyone thinks he's cute. He's just a younger, screamier, dribblier version of Bub Tub.

Mandy is moody. She doesn't have a thing to say in or out of class. Gretta is very protective and won't let her out of her sight. She even waits for Mandy outside the toilet block, and if I so much as open my mouth she says, "I'm going to whack you, Danny

Thompson, if you say anything to upset her."

When I wake up the next day the house is rattling as if it's been taken over by a family of spooks. I tumble out of bed, press my nose to the window and watch the tree outside do a weird dance as it sways this way and that.

"It's the Southerly Buster," Dad says over breakfast. "The good weather couldn't last forever."

On the way to school I notice that all the trees in the street are flopping their branches around.

All morning the wind blows. The windows shake. The classroom door creaks.

Corky whispers to me, "It's Casper the ghost knocking. Should I let him in?"

Mandy sits very still at her desk with her hands clasped in front of her. Her face is pale. I feel worried. She seems so stressed out.

Mr King says to us, "Now, class, we're going to cut across the school yard and go to the library. Stay together—a few branches have already come off some of the trees in the grounds. As you've probably noticed it's a very windy day."

When he says that Taffy makes a very squeaky, rude noise. Mr King glares and looks around the classroom.

"Who did that?"

We all laugh, even Mandy. Eventually Mr King has no choice but to give up waiting for Taffy to own up. He tells us to stand up, file out the classroom, and follow him across the yard to the library.

As we walk out of the classroom he says, "Corky why is your jaw bouncing around? Are you chewing gum again?"

Corky, who is walking beside me, gulps and swallows his gum in a hurry.

"No, Mr King. The only thing inside my mouth is spit."

"Thank you, Corky. I get the point. Now stay in line and be quiet."

We troop across the yard. The wind is whistling. Clouds are darting across the sky like rocket ships.

The library is a grey, serious-looking building just next to the canteen. I look around to see where Mandy is. She's at the very end of the long line of kids from our class. I slow down and wait for her. She's with her Siamese twin, Gretta.

Suddenly I see Mandy roughly pushing Gretta to one side. Gretta loses her balance and falls over. She sits in a collapsed heap, staring up at Mandy in amazement. A roof tile lands just beside her. Gretta points to the tile. Her hand is shaking.

"Mandy, why did you ... hey, that tile could have hit me. I could have died."

48

"I saw it drop from the roof," says Mandy. She kneels beside Gretta. "Are you OK?"

Mr King has meantime come back to see what all the fuss is about.

"Mandy pushed me out of the way just in time," squeaks Gretta to Mr King as she slowly gets to her feet. "That tile came right off the roof. I could have died."

Mr King shakes his head. "Good gracious. It's just as well you saw that tile coming, Mandy. Now I want you to all get away from here quickly in case other tiles fall. I'll organise for workmen to come out and fix the roof immediately. Join up with the class and file into the library."

"Hey, Mandy," I say as we troop along. "If you hadn't worn your glasses I reckon you wouldn't have seen that tile."

She shrugs her shoulders. But there's a tiny smile on her face. "Maybe," she says.

"He's right," says Gretta and her voice is still squeaky with shock. "Your glasses saved my life."

"I don't know about that," says Mandy modestly.

"Sure," I say, because I'm on a roll now. "Gretta might have ended up with her brains splattered all over the school yard. Not that it would have made much of a mess."

"Shut up, Danny Thompson, or I'll whack you,"

says Gretta.

Mandy's smile is now like a tiny new moon.

I quickly look around to check that Corky and Taffy are out of earshot.

"Also, I reckon those glasses make you, um, um, pretty. Sort of. Your eyes. Um. Well, they sort of look bluer in those frames."

I start to feel hot and cold.

Gretta stares at Mandy. It's as if she's seeing her for the first time.

"Danny Thompson's an idiot, but even an idiot is right once in a while. Your eyes *do* look bluer. Funny how I hadn't noticed it before."

Mandy's small white teeth are showing. Her smile is growing bigger and bigger.

"You at the end. Stop dawdling!" screams Mr King from the library entrance.

"You know, Mandy," says Gretta. "I just can't understand how I missed seeing that tile fall. Maybe I need glasses too. I reckon I'll get my eyes checked out. Do you think I'd look good in glasses? I saw this ad on television. It was that top model. Elle something or another. She was wearing these really cool glasses. She looked so beautiful. You saved my life, Mandy. You're my very best friend. Do you know if you save someone's life it means you've got to be friends forever? I reckon that's the way we'll be …"

We walk into the library.

"Why are you smiling?" Corky asks me as we are shown a display of posters and books.

I just can't tell him.

Ear Today, Gone Tomorrow

It was bad enough when Taffy kept pulling his hair out. That steady pluck, pluck, pluck was like the slow dripping of a tap.

My nerves were like bits of jangled wire. However, Taffy tried to be considerate. He stopped plucking his hair and methodically began to tug his left ear lobe.

For a long time I ignored it. I reckoned anything had to be better than hair-pulling.

Finally, though, he's worn me down. If you go down

to the beach you'll see that the rocks are curved and pitted. Dad once told me that's where the waves have swished against them for millions of years, slowly eating them away.

Taffy is having the same effect on me. Tug, tug, tug. It goes on and on. He's not driving just me nuts. It's affecting everyone.

More missiles are thrown at Taffy in class than anyone else. Everything from pencils to yesterday's lunch. Even Mr King can't stand it.

"Taffy Douglas. Kindly stop tugging your ear lobe and concentrate on your work."

"Taffy Douglas. Leave your ear lobe alone."

"Taffy Douglas. If you don't stop that I'm going to, going to ..."

This last remark is a waste of time, because it doesn't matter what Mr King threatens. The lobe-pulling stays.

"The thing is," I say to Corky over lunch one day, "he's not going to quit until he solves his problem."

"If his parents want to move he can't do anything about it." Corky bites into his peanut butter sandwich. "I vote we get him to take up a new habit. Maybe he can scratch the palm of his hand when he gets nervous."

"That's a thought," I say. I watch Taffy as he walks across the playground. He's holding his lunch with one hand and frantically pulling his ear lobe with the other.

That weekend Taffy phones me and asks me to come over. His parents have bought him a new bike.

"Hey, that's awesome. What's the occasion?"

"It's a bribe. That's the occasion. It's to cheer me up and keep me away from the house while it's up for sale. The real estate agent's bringing people over this afternoon and my parents don't want me hanging around tugging my ear. I don't want the stupid bike. I just want to stay put."

I nick over to Taffy's house after lunch. There's a sign in his front garden just near the letterbox. "FOR SALE. Immaculate 3-bedroom home. Apply Fieldings Real Estate." The phone number of the real estate agent is underneath.

Taffy is riding a great-looking bike down the driveway. The bike is very cool with shiny red handlebars. The best thing about it is that it keeps Taffy's hands away from his ear.

"Great bike," I call out to him. Taffy cycles slowly and miserably towards me.

"Don't care," he says. We go into his garden where he parks the bike by the side tap.

"Don't care about anything," says Taffy. "Come inside. You should see how tidy everything is. We've

54

got some creepy people coming to see the house in half an hour. Mum's running around polishing everything. Dad's fixed up all the light fittings so they're not leaning on one side. The house looks so good. And now they want to sell it."

Taffy and I go inside. Sure enough there's Mrs Douglas holding a can of air freshener.

"Hallo, Danny. Wipe your feet on the mat and don't touch anything. If you boys get food from the kitchen don't leave a mess. I want everything to look just so."

"Just so," repeats Taffy while I rub my shoes on the door mat. "Did you hear that?"

We go into Taffy's bedroom. His room is really neat. It looks like something out of a magazine. I reckon if I ran my finger along his bookshelf there wouldn't even be enough dust there to give Bub Tub a decent meal.

"Here's my footy cards," says Taffy. He gets a heap of cards from inside his desk. I squat on the carpet and try to look at them, but it's hard to concentrate. Taffy's sitting on the end of his bed, pulling his ear lobe. The air freshener is going to make me sneeze. I'd like a drink or some ice-cream, but Mrs Douglas may make a scene about the way it messes up the neatness of her kitchen.

"You see," Taffy's saying, "Dad's got a chance to

get a transfer to Adelaide. He's assistant manager of his company here, but if he goes to Adelaide they'll train him to be manager. He reckons this is a good time to make changes. Nobody thinks about me."

"Adelaide. That's a long way away."

"I'd have to go to a new school and make new friends. I don't want to do that."

Just then the doorbell rings. Taffy turns pale.

"It's those creepy people come to see our house. What's wrong with them? Don't they have their own house? Why can't they leave us alone?"

I fumble with Taffy's footy cards and listen to garbled voices and the tread of shoes as people plod through the hall.

There's a short, sharp knock on the door and it opens wide. A small man with a round shiny face says to the couple with him, "This is the second bedroom. It's very roomy with a built-in wardrobe along that wall. It's nice and airy too."

I don't know how the real estate agent can say this as the room stinks of Mrs Douglas's air freshener. The man and woman walk into Taffy's bedroom. They nod at Taffy and me, but otherwise ignore us. They walk around the room, tap the wall and look out the window.

"Lovely," says the lady. "It would make a nice bedroom for our Cecily."

The real estate man's face becomes even shinier. Suddenly, Taffy pipes up.

"It's a pity that we've got white ants in the house. And the roof leaks all the time. Especially when it rains. And the cockroaches. We keep spraying, but they keep coming back. It's to do with the way the house was built and the cracks in the walls."

The shiny-faced man gives a kind of sick laugh. "Ha ha, that boy will carry on. What a joker."

The woman grabs her husband's arm. She says to Taffy, "White ants, you say? And the roof leaks?" She turns to her husband. "It's a very old house. We could be up for a lot of expense, Arthur."

The real estate agent says quickly, "Hey, the boy's kidding around. Tell them, Taffy. Tell them you were just joking."

But it is too late. The couple shake their heads, give the walls one more nervous tap with their hands, then leave.

Not long after they've gone, Taffy's mother comes running in to the room.

"Taffy, Mr Jiggins the real estate man told me you ruined the sale. Those people were really interested. How could you tell them such lies? White ants? Cockroaches? What's wrong with you? And leave that ear alone!"

After his mother has gone, Taffy smiles at me.

"Not bad, hey? All I have to do is hang around when people come to see the house and I can talk them out of buying it."

I think about this. "It'll only work if you're home. What if someone comes to see the house and you're at school? You can't be here all the time."

Taffy's face droops. "You're right. I've got to have a proper plan."

He stares out of his window for a long time while I sort through his footy cards.

"I know," he says suddenly, and his eyes are like two bright torches.

He hops off his bed and goes to his desk. He takes a few sheets of paper and a pen and sits down next to me on the carpet.

"The local paper has a section on interesting houses. Do you know how old my house is?"

"It's so shiny today it looks like it was built last week."

"My house is over one hundred years old," says Taffy proudly. "Bushrangers used to hold up coaches round this area. Willy Wibflunger was the worst. He was a kind of Robin Hood. Except that he stole from the rich and gave it all to himself. He killed a few people too if they didn't hand over their jewels and money quick fast. My family's heavily into the past. Don't you know your history?"

"I know that until the corner shop opened up, there was nowhere to buy decent bubblegum."

Taffy ignores this and carries on. "I'm going to write the local paper a letter. I reckon it's very important that the whole neighbourhood knows that my house is haunted, don't you?"

I grin. This is sounding cool.

We sit and plot the letter. Little frowns of concentration wriggle around like worms on Taffy's forehead. We write and cross out. We use up fourteen sheets of paper. Finally we come up with this.

Dear Editor,

I thought that your readers might like to know about the house I live in. It's genuinly hauntid. Here is some information about it.

Taffy leaves a gap, then writes:

Some of your readers may know about the notorios Willy Wibflunger, the local bushranger who a hundred years ago used to rob stage coaches and murder people. 24 Wilson Street, Appleby, looks nice now. There are roses growing where the bodies once were burid. But on dark nights the ghosts of those shot people still walk the garden and rooms of the house wailing "Willy Wibflunger did this to me."

Mr & Mrs Douglas and their son Taffy live at Number 24. They are trying to sell their house in a hurry. Why? Could it be because they're sick of living in a hauntid house?

I grin as I read the letter. "That's great, Taffy, but you can see that a kid's written this, and I'm not sure about some of the spelling."

"No worries," says Taffy. "I'll nick into Dad's study and use his computer. This is going to look very cool by the time I've finished."

Taffy's dad's study is another very neat room smelling like a pine forest. Taffy types out his letter on the computer and checks his spelling. Finally he prints out an awesome, professional-looking letter.

Taffy checks the address of the local newspaper in the telephone book, writes it on an envelope and pinches a stamp from the top drawer of the desk.

"I'll post it on my way home," I tell him.

I put the letter in my pocket, then we go into the kitchen and help ourselves to chocolate ice-cream.

Taffy's dad walks into the room.

"Your mother told me what you said to those people, Taffy. Why don't you want us to sell the house? We'll buy a lovely home in Adelaide. Maybe we'll even be able to get one with a swimming pool. You'll make lots of new friends."

"I don't want new friends," says Taffy through a mouthful of ice-cream. "I want my old friends. I don't want to move."

He pulls at his ear with his free hand. Taffy's father looks very annoyed. "Taffy, leave your ear alone. And don't interfere with the sale of the house again. Promise?"

Taffy crosses his fingers behind his ear and says, "Sure."

After I've finished my ice-cream I leave. I post Taffy's letter at the corner post box. When I get home Bub Tub is sitting in the back yard in her baby swimming pool. It is a good idea not to get splashed by the water she's paddling in because she wees non-stop in it.

"Ayo, Anny," she waves to me.

"G'day, Bub Tub," I say, standing well back.

Mum is digging near some small plants. I look around the garden. Funny how you take your home for granted. I've never thought about what it would be like to move.

"We'll never leave this house, will we, Mum?"

Mum wipes her forehead with one hand and squints at me. "Who can say, Danny? We're certainly not planning to move."

I stare into space. Imagine if Dad got offered a supermarket, not just a small deli, but a kingsize supermarket in Queensland. We'd move into a grand house with a pool and tennis court maybe, and Bub Tub could have her own baby pool, complete with a sewer pipe.

I'd get lots of video games. We'd go out to dinner, and maybe during school holidays we'd go to exciting places like Spain and Antarctica.

"Danny are you listening to me?" It's Mum. "This is the third time I'm asking you—do you have any homework?"

Two days later Taffy runs over to Corky and me in the school yard.

"I've got some great news."

"What? Are you going to stop tugging your ear?" asks Corky.

"I won't have to pull my ear any more. I won't have any nervous habits because we won't be moving. The newspaper is going to print the story."

"What story?" asks Corky. I quickly fill him in.

Taffy jumps around impatiently. When he speaks his voice is squeaky with excitement.

"They phoned from the *Weekly Courier*. They got that letter I sent and wanted to check if the story was genuine. Mum and Dad were talking to the real estate agent so I took the call. They asked lots of questions about Willy Wibflunger. I told them how he'd been caught and hanged, but he still comes back to haunt the house some nights. He stomps through the hall and we can't get to sleep. They said they're going to drive by and take a picture of the house. Imagine. Our house is famous. The story's coming out on Saturday."

"This is great," says Corky. "Almost as good as the time Helen the Horrible swallowed a fly."

A few days later Dad brings in the local paper. He's whistling to himself. Suddenly he stops whistling and starts laughing.

"The ghost of Willy Wibflunger. Ha ha ha."

He spreads the newspaper on the kitchen table. I run across and peer at it.

There on the front page is a picture of the Douglas house. Beside it is Taffy's letter. Someone at the newspaper has drawn a cartoon impression of Willy in a cowboy hat, waving two guns around. There is also an article by a reporter.

"Taffy Douglas told us how he'd witnessed the ghostly walking of Willy Wibflunger in his home and in the back garden above his mother's rose bed," I read.

Taffy can be proud of himself.

A few hours later the phone rings. Mum calls, "It's for you, Danny. It's Taffy."

He's very excited. "Have you seen the newspaper? My parents are going nuts. The real estate agent's going nuts. He reckons no one will want to buy our house now it's haunted."

Taffy stops, take a big breath and starts again.

"Some weirdos are walking around our front garden right now saying they can feel the vibes of spirits. Mum's put the hose on them twice, but they keep coming back. This is a very cool situation. And you know, I don't even *want* to touch my ear lobe. I reckon I'm cured."

"Do your parents want to kill you?" I ask.

"It's too late for that. I'm dead meat already," says Taffy. "They don't think it's funny at all. They've asked the newspaper to print something to say they made a big mistake. I think it's called a retraction. But it doesn't matter. Dad says the damage has been done. He says we won't sell the house for years and he can't take on that new job unless the house is sold. I reckon I'm some kind of genius."

As the days roll by, 24 Wilson Street turns into a top tourist attraction. A priest asks Taffy's parents if they want him to get rid of the ghosts. It's called exorcising and has nothing to do with push-ups. Taffy asks his mother if he can conduct guided tours around the rose beds where the bodies are buried. She just

64

manages to stop herself from throttling him.

Then, out of the blue, when Taffy is up there riding a cool blue wave through the ocean, when nothing can go wrong …

"Something terrible has happened." It's Taffy on the phone.

"What?"

"We've been robbed."

"What are you talking about?"

"Last night I couldn't sleep," says Taffy. "Also I was hungry. I woke up and decided I'd see what was in the fridge. I got out of bed and I heard this noise. I thought maybe we had mice.

"Anyway, I walked through the hall. I saw this funny light coming from the lounge room. It was spooky. I saw this shadow. And then a man. He looked at me, then jumped back into the shadows. Don't laugh at me—the light was sort of jumping around him and his face was pale and I could have sworn it was Willy Wibflunger."

"That's nuts. Willy? What happened next?"

"I crept back into bed. I was so nervous. The house went quiet and I reckoned he'd gone. You know, crawled back into his open grave.

"Anyway, I must have dozed off and the next thing I heard was Mum screaming, 'We've been robbed!' I jumped out of bed and the house looked like it had been hit by a tornado. The video had gone and our TV and lots of other things. Some money that was lying around went too. And Mum's jewellery. The police have been here. My parents are nervous wrecks.

"When I told my mum and dad that I'd actually come face to face with the burglar and then gone back to bed they completely freaked."

"Are you grounded forever?"

"I don't think I'll be allowed out to play until I'm seventy-three." Taffy pauses, then says, "Danny, you don't reckon it could have been Willy Wibflunger? The guy looked really spooky."

"What would a ghost want with the family silver?"

"Maybe a ghost has a way of turning it into ghost silver," says Taffy. "I mean, if it *was* Willy, then I'm really living in a haunted house. I don't want to live in a haunted house. I'm starting to feel scared."

"You're not going to start tugging your ear again, are you?"

There is this long pause. Then Taffy says, "No, but I've got this funny, itchy feeling under both my arms."

Oh no!

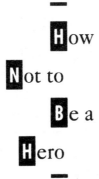

How Not to Be a Hero

I watch the boy on TV. He jumped in a river and saved his baby brother from drowning. It was an awesome thing to do. The water was deep and his brother had wandered away from their parents who were setting up a barbie for their picnic lunch.

If the boy hadn't saved his brother it would have been a terrible picnic, that's for sure. Now he's being presented with a medal by the Prime Minister. Nice things are being said about him. The boy looks pleased with himself. His parents are standing near him. His mother is holding the baby brother who looks very bored.

After the presentation, Dad turns off the TV.

"That boy was so brave," he says. "What a kid!"

Mum, who is sitting on the sofa, bouncing Bub Tub on her knee, smiles. "You're right, Roger. He's a real hero."

I sit there watching my parents and thinking. I've never done anything really brave. I've saved Bub Tub on a million occasions from eating beetles and caterpillars. But that's not real hero stuff. I've steadied the ladder for Dad when he's been fixing the drainpipes and for sure if I hadn't steadied it he'd have been a goner.

Then there was this kid, Bert, at school who was being picked on by other kids. I stood in front of him when these big bullies came to punch him. I threatened them with ten different karate chops. I couldn't do them but I'd seen them in the video of *The Karate Kid*. I reckon I saved Bert. But then I found out he'd been pinching the other kids' lunch and pocket money and maybe he wasn't worth saving.

It would be nice to be a fair dinkum hero. To be given a medal by the Prime Minister. To have everyone clapping and saying what a beaut kid I was.

I spin out of these thoughts as our doorbell rings.

"That must be one of our neighbours for the

meeting," says Dad. He gets up from his armchair and opens the front door. I remember then. Mum and Dad are having a Neighbourhood Watch meeting. It's on account of the crime in Sydney. Apart from the robbery at Taffy's house there have been break-ins in other streets, and everyone is worried. So our neighbours are meeting at our place to discuss how we can keep an eye (or two) on each other's property.

"Come in, Mr Williams," I can hear Dad saying. Mr Williams lives three houses down. He's an old guy with silver hair and mean blue eyes. He has a bad temper. One of my cricket balls went through his front window. You should have seen the way he carried on. He did a little tap dance and said, "Danny Thompson, you're going to pay for this."

I did, too, out of my pocket money. Then, a few weeks ago, I was zooming around the street on my skateboard. Mr Williams was holding a bag of groceries in the middle of the pathway as I came tearing past. I didn't even touch him, but he somehow overbalanced and fell. He hurt his foot. It wasn't my fault. He sent a rude note to my parents saying how he didn't feel safe in his own street with me around.

Now, he's sitting at the dining table with Mum, while Dad puts Bub Tub to bed.

"Neighbourhood Watch is an excellent idea," he's saying to Mum. "We need to look out for each other."

Then he spies me. "Hallo, Danny," he says stiffly.

"G'day, Mr Williams," I say politely. "How's the foot?"

Mr Williams's lips twist into a very unkind sneer. Before he has a chance to say anything the doorbell rings. Within ten minutes the dining room is filled with our neighbours. Mum and Dad hand out tea and biscuits while the discussion goes on.

I go into the kitchen and pour myself a cold drink. Then I bring a kitchen stool to the dining room and sit by the door and listen to them.

"It's very simple," says Dad. "We've just got to be more alert. If, say, one of us goes on holiday we should let other people in the street know, so they can watch the house."

"Hear hear."

"We should also be aware if anything unusual happens. For instance, if a neighbour hasn't said anything about moving and we see a big truck outside a home with men loading furniture, well, that's a good reason to be suspicious."

"Specially if they're wearing masks and carrying guns," I call out.

Ten heads turn towards me. No one thinks I'm funny.

"Danny, ah, don't you have some homework to do?" says Mum.

I get up and leave. I know when I'm not wanted.

I go to my bedroom. I hear noises from Bub Tub's room. I steal quietly into her bedroom. Bub Tub is lying on her back in her cot. She's having a wonderful conversation with the red-and-blue clown mobile hanging from the ceiling.

"Ah doozy. Ba phlud. Iggle bug," she says.

Then she sees me at the door. "Ayo Anny."

I walk over to her. When Bub Tub's lying on her back in the cot with a clean nappy she's almost bearable. Her cheeks are fat and pink and at this moment she's not even dribbling.

If Bub Tub was in trouble there'd be no two ways about it. I'd be there to save her. I don't think that boy on TV did anything so special. Saving a sister or brother is just a natural thing to do. Imagine if he hadn't saved him. If he'd just stayed by the river bank calling out to his brother, "Swim, you fool." Everyone would have been horrified. He had to save his brother and be a hero, or let him sink and be a coward.

I have a shower, finish my homework, read a few comics and go to bed. I can still hear them yapping in the dining room.

"We'll create Safe Houses. You know, put up those signs in our front gardens that the Police Department give out. That way kids who are lost or being followed have a safe house to go to."

"That's a fine idea," Mum says.

I can see it now. Every nervous kid in New South Wales will end up in our house. But they'll only ever come once. Ten minutes with Bub Tub's stink will fix them up. Then someone will change the sign to "Unsafe House".

The next day on the way to school I see Mr Williams crossing the road. Normally I'd avoid him. But he's old and slow, and though he's crossing at the traffic lights, there's no way he's going to make it before the lights change. And there are all those angry cars snorting like rhinos. They'll knock him down. He'll be left like minced droppings on the road. I'd better do the right thing. Also, it's practice for being a hero.

I run to where Mr Williams is methodically making his way across the street. The sign is already flashing "Don't Walk". He'll be in serious trouble if I don't do something. I hold up one arm to let the traffic know I've just become a kind of citizen traffic cop. I use my other arm to guide Mr Williams across the road. This is very cool. He will be so grateful.

It is very sad but as I reach out to help Mr Williams, I manage to knock him off balance. He tries to steady himself, but he's leaning this way and that. The lights have already changed. Traffic is snarling.

I try to steady Mr Williams, but it is too late. He wobbles, then falls.

I try to help him to his feet. He waves me away.

"Danny Thompson. You're a disaster."

"Hold on," I say. "I was just trying to help you."

But Mr Williams is dead angry. His face has turned a funny shade of red and he's pointing his finger at me in a threatening way. Also the racket coming from the honking of cars is very unreasonable. All the cars are piled up in one angry line while Mr Williams gets to his feet. By the time he is standing, the lights have turned red for the oncoming traffic and the cars have to stop anyway.

Mr Williams walks as quickly as he can across the road. I follow him, checking that he doesn't lose his balance, because there is still a chance I could save him.

A few days later I'm waiting at the shopping centre to catch a bus to the library. The bank is nearby. I casually watch all the people going in and coming out.

I see a young guy. He's wearing a striped T-shirt and shorts and has a baseball cap on his head turned back to front. He is carrying something long in a large brown paper bag. Is it possible …? No. Yet the shape is about right. And the guy has shifty eyes. And thin lips. And a scab over his left eyebrow.

I stand there sweating. It just could be. On the other hand …

I do the right thing. I run up to the enquiry desk and tell the lady behind it, "See that man over there in the striped T-shirt? I think he could be carrying a gun."

The lady at the desk freaks out. Blobs of sweat appear on her forehead as she whispers, "Good grief. Are you sure?"

If she would only wait for my answer I know I would say, "Not absolutely sure." But she doesn't wait. She must have pressed an alarm because two security guards appear quicker than Clark Kent getting on his Superman gear.

The lady tells them what I've said. They push quickly through the crowd of people and grab the guy in the queue. Everyone in the bank looks terrified, particularly the man who is being grabbed. I start to think.

They'll write about me in the newspapers. About how alert I am. How I'd noticed something odd about the man. Mum and Dad will be so proud of me.

While I am thinking this, the security men open the guy's brown paper bag. Three long cucumbers fall out.

The blobs of sweat on the forehead of the lady at the enquiry desk immediately dry. She looks at me.

Her teeth are very big and some of the things she says to me are not really nice. I run out of the bank as quickly as I can.

This business of becoming a hero is starting to wear me out. I decide to give the whole thing a rest.

A week later, after I've been playing cricket at the park, I make my way home. I walk past the old church hall. It's used for all kinds of things. The scouts meet there, and there's a local ballet school that has classes there too.

I am just passing the front of the building when I hear voices. They are very loud.

"Don't … please, don't. Put that knife away."

"I warned you, Charlie. I told you if you spilled the beans to the cops that would be it. You had your chance."

"No … look, I'll leave the State. I'll leave Australia. Please, I've got a family."

"Don't kill him. Please … don't," a woman's voice pleads.

Every pore in my body turns into a major goose-bump. The hair on my head prickles. This can't be happening.

"You shouldn't have squealed. You know what we do to squealers."

I hear a moan. I have to do something. This is for real. Those are real voices. There's a phone box right across the road. I must call the police. I just hope I won't be too late.

I dial 000, the emergency number. In the time it takes for me to blink I am connected to a deep voice which says, "Sergeant Grey here. What seems to be the matter?"

I quickly tell him what I have heard. I tell him where the church hall is. The sergeant sounds very impressed with me.

"This could be serious, young man. You stay well away from the hall. We'll have a few of our chaps there in no time."

I hang around near the phone box. Maybe it's too late. Maybe the guy, Charlie, has been knifed already. Maybe his guts are spilled all over the floor. Maybe the girls who come for their ballet lessons will end up sliding around on the blood.

I wait, shivering. Suddenly two police cars pull up outside the hall. Two policemen get out of each car. I walk nervously across the road to them.

"I made the call," I say to one policeman. He is tall, fairly young and very solid looking.

"Good boy," he says. "Now the voices were coming from inside the hall, is that right?"

I nod. The policeman tells me to wait behind the telephone box. I move away, shaking so much I think I have goosebumps on my goosebumps.

Standing well back, I see the policemen walk cautiously to the hall door. One of them quickly opens it. Four policemen spring inside with their guns raised. I listen. No shots are fired. That's a good sign. I can hear a few loud voices, but I can't make out what's being said.

The policemen walk out of the church hall. They've put away their guns. They are accompanied by two men and one woman. Good, they've caught them. Then I notice that one of the men looks suspiciously like Mr Williams.

A policeman calls out to me. "Hey you, I want to have a talk with you."

I run across the road. I am a hero. A top-of-the-range, first-class hero. Still, imagine our very own Mr Williams being part of some underworld set-up. And he looks so harmless. Just goes to show how you can never be sure of anyone.

I notice that the policeman's face is red and twitching. Why?

"These people were rehearsing for a play," he says. "The local drama society meets here every week. You've wasted our time, young man. What did you say your name was again?"

I stand there speechless, but Mr Williams isn't speechless.

"His name is Danny Thompson. Number One

Neighbourhood Nuisance," he says. Then he goes on to say other things about me which are quite hurtful.

I leave the area as quickly as possible. I'm giving up on this hero stuff. I'm going to concentrate on being a top wimp.

I run all the way home, just stopping for a moment to help some small, screaming kid get his teddy bear's ear out of the jaws of a cat.

Later, while I'm looking at the pattern of my wallpaper as I try to get stuck into my homework, Mum walks in.

"Danny, I've just had a phone call from Mrs Lee down the road." Mum's face is as happy as a smiley stamp.

"Huh?"

"She said that you rescued her grandson's teddy bear's ear from the neighbour's cat."

"Big deal."

"Danny, it was a nice thing to do. And brave too. That's a crazy cat. He could have hurt you."

"Really?"

"Mrs Lee wants you to drop by tomorrow. She's baking you a special chocolate cake. I'm proud of you, Danny."

So, there you go.

It looks like I'm a hero after all.

I'm not your jumbo-sized hero who develops a

vaccine to save the world from a killer virus.

I'm not your king-sized hero who pulls a child away from the path of an oncoming train.

I'm just a teeny hero who rescues teddy bear ears.

Well, it's a start.

Dead
Worried

I am dead worried. Everything is going wrong. This has been a very bad week.

Firstly, I have dandruff. This is very off. It has been settling on my navy school shirt like drifts of snow. Then Dad brought home a stuffed parrot on a perch. He thinks it is a great art form. I think it's enough to give a spook nightmares. Also, Bub Tub is covered in spots. Mum says it's an allergy, but she could be wrong. It could be contagious. I could end up with dandruff *and* spots. Even worse, I may develop spot dandruff, a new and rare form of dandruff where each grain of dandruff has a red spot in the middle of it.

I'm carrying on like this because I am very stressed out. You see, I haven't come to what is really making me dead worried.

I think I'm adopted.

I don't think I'd have paid any attention to Mum and Dad's conversation if it hadn't been for Gretta Licz.

It all began last week.

It was lunchtime. Taffy, Corky and I were sitting on the grass swapping sandwiches. Gretta was sprawled out nearby with Mandy.

I could hear them yapping to each other. Gretta has this huge voice.

"I don't mind being adopted," she was saying. "In some ways it's better. *You* just happened to come along. *I* was chosen."

She said this in a very smug voice. I called out to her, "Do you ever want to meet your real parents?"

Gretta turned her nose up at me. She doesn't like boys very much. I've heard her say to Mandy that we smell, which isn't fair because I'm sure she pongs from time to time like the rest of us.

"I *have* my real parents. Your parents are the ones who are there for you when you need them. My mum and dad have always been there for me. They were the ones who took me to hospital to have my tonsils out. And they were there for me when I cut

81

my knee and got that big scab with the pus oozing out. And when I swallowed the top of my pen …"

"Yeah, all right, Gretta. But what about the parents who *had* you. You know what I mean. Do you ever want to meet them?"

"You mean my birth parents? I get curious sometimes. Maybe when I'm older I'll put my name down on a special register and try to find them. I've always known I was adopted so maybe that's why I feel comfortable with it. I reckon it'd be hard to find out suddenly though." Gretta wrinkled her nose. "You've got dirt on your sandwich, Taffy."

"So what," said Taffy. "It just gives it more flavour." He bit into his sandwich while Corky and I cheered.

After school when Corky and I were dawdling along Mulberry Lane I said to him, "I wonder what Gretta's parents look like. I wonder if her birth mother has brown hair and brown eyes like Gretta. I wonder if she's a pain like Gretta."

Corky said, "I wish that Helen the Horrible was adopted and her birth parents suddenly turned up and demanded that we give her back. That would be so cool."

When I arrived home I found Mum in the kitchen shaking her head. Bub Tub was sitting on the floor talking to Uggle Bee, her favourite doll.

On the kitchen table was a horrible-looking stuffed

parrot on a wooden perch. It had long feathers and big poppy eyes, and its beak was curled into a mad grin.

Mum was frowning at it.

"Someone came around to your dad's shop and sold him this monstrosity. Your father likes it."

The stuffed parrot had to be the ugliest thing this side of the southern hemisphere.

Bub Tub liked it though. She stood up and showed Uggle Bee the parrot. "Ook Uggle Bee. Irdy."

"Where are you going to put it?" I asked Mum. "What about at the back of the broom cupboard?"

"I can't, Danny. Your father is really taken with it. He used to have a parrot called Polly when he was a boy and he says Polly looked just like this. He's very stubborn about it. He wants to put it somewhere special." Mum shuddered.

"It's pretty gross," I said. "I guess I take after you in taste, huh, Mum?"

"What's that, Danny? Yes, I guess you do."

Mum hummed and haaed. She didn't know what to do with the bird.

"Why don't you put it in Bub Tub's room? You can tell Dad how much Bub Tub loves it."

Mum beamed at me. "That's an excellent idea. I'm surprised I didn't think of it before. And it's the truth. Bub Tub does love it."

"I guess she takes after Dad, huh?"

"I suppose she does, Danny," said Mum. She patted my head and seemed very pleased. With Bub Tub holding Uggle Bee and toddling after us, we took the gross parrot into Bub Tub's room and put it on top of her little white cupboard. It sat there on its perch, grinning insanely.

Bub Tub jumped up and down in excitement.

"Ook, Uggle Bee," she said. "Ook. Pitty irdy."

I didn't know if Bub Tub was saying the parrot was good looking or it was a pity it had been put in her room.

When Dad came home from work he kept going into Bub Tub's bedroom and saying things like, "Want a cracker, Polly?" And although I knew he was just carrying on because the bird reminded him of his long-lost parrot, I was seriously worried about him.

"Can't we find a more prominent spot for Polly to sit than Bub Tub's bedroom?" he asked Mum during dinner.

"She just loves having that bird in her room," said Mum quickly, and when Dad began to serve the vegetables she winked at me.

The next morning just before I left for school Mum said, "Hey, I think you've got dandruff."

She pointed to my shoulders. I looked at my shirt and sure enough there were tiny white flakes there.

"Hmm," said Mum. "I'd better have a good look

at your scalp." She grabbed me and started to pull my hair apart. "Just checking for nits, Danny," she told me.

Nits! I freaked out. I'd had them once and the whole family had to have their hair fumigated. Luckily this time Mum said, "No worries. It's just dandruff. Your hair's full of it. It's to do with getting older. I'll get you a medicated shampoo."

I wasn't really worried about the dandruff, but at school the next day Gretta noticed the white spots on my shirt.

"Hey, look at him. He's got nits crawling all over him. Yuk."

This was not a very nice thing to say. Mandy frowned and moved back slightly. I had to do a lot of explaining about the difference between nits parachuting onto my shirt and plain old dandruff. I started to feel embarrassed and decided that it'd be a good thing if Mum bought some anti-dandruff stuff for me because I didn't want Mandy running away when she saw me. I didn't want that at all.

All this brings me up to Wednesday. When I got home from school I found Mum rubbing lotion into Bub Tub's skin.

"Bubby's come out in all these spots," she told me. "I think it must be an allergy. She's been eating a lot of strawberries lately. It might be that."

When I asked Mum about the dandruff shampoo she said, "It's in the bathroom. I only bought a mild shampoo. I hope it's strong enough to do the trick."

I washed my hair. The shampoo, which smelt foul, did not do the trick. It just seemed to loosen the dandruff. When my hair dried there was more dandruff than ever flaking onto my shoulders. This was very off.

"I'll get you something stronger tomorrow," promised Mum. "Don't worry."

Dad had just arrived home. "Hey, Dad," I said as he walked into the kitchen. "Did you get dandruff when you were my age?"

"No, can't say that I did," Dad said.

"What about you, Mum?"

"I didn't get it either."

"I always did say you were one of a kind," chuckled Dad. "Anyway, don't worry. We'll get rid of it."

I told Dad that I wasn't worried, but really I didn't want Mandy Miller turning pale with fright when she saw me and my dandruff.

After dinner, when Bub Tub was talking to herself in her cot, I sat at my desk in my bedroom and did my maths homework. Halfway through I got bored and decided to get some ice-cream from the kitchen.

As I walked past the lounge room I heard Mum and Dad talking.

"I don't know, Roger," Mum was saying. "I guess we should have told Danny earlier. He's going to get upset."

"I hope he'll take it well," Dad said. "It'll be hard for him. Still …"

I stood behind the lounge room door. I heard some muffled sounds then Mum said, "It's not the end of the world. I'll talk to him in a few days. When did you say she was coming?"

That was all I heard because just then Bub Tub started crying and Dad jumped up to go to her.

I nicked off into the kitchen and sat down, thinking. What were my parents on about? What was this big thing they were worried about telling me? It was then I remembered about Gretta being adopted.

I thought about myself then. I had reddish-brown hair and seventeen freckles. I was just a dead average kid. Dad had brown hair and an ordinary face, but I didn't really look like him. Mum's hair was fairer and her eyes were light. As she was a bit plump I didn't resemble her either. I definitely didn't look anything like Bub Tub.

I started to feel my skin twitch. Could I be … was it possible that I was … adopted?

That conversation my parents just had. What were they really saying?

They had something to tell me. I might not take it

well. Some woman was coming over. Who? My birth mother, that's who! The one who had put me up for adoption all those years ago. The one I looked like. A dead average mother with reddish-brown hair and seventeen freckles on her face.

I began to feel sick. Maybe she'd bring my birth father. He'd have dandruff on his shirt. That's how I'd recognise him. Maybe his socks would have an unbearable stink coming from them. Wasn't it just the other day that Dad said to me, "Danny, your socks stink. I don't know why your feet smell so bad. Mine never smell like that."

What did all this mean?

I feel terrible. I should go straight up to Mum and Dad and say, "Hey, I heard you two talking last night. The game's up."

But then I might do something really dumb like start to cry and babble about how I'll always love them even if they aren't my birth parents ...

The new dandruff shampoo worked and the dandruff got washed down the drain. My hair now smells like a hospital toilet.

Bub Tub's body is still covered with spots. She looks terrible. I am dead worried that she's contagious, and I keep well away from her.

Dad continues to visit the daggy parrot in her bedroom and talk daggy talk to it.

Occasionally I catch Mum staring at me, but she doesn't say a word about the woman who is supposed to be coming.

I corner Gretta Licz at school. "Gretta, do you feel your parents love you any less because you're adopted?"

"Phew," says Gretta. "You smell like a ..."

"A hospital toilet. Yes, I know," I say. "It's my dandruff shampoo. Forget that. I need to know whether your parents love you just the same as if they really had you."

"What's it to you?" says Gretta.

"I'm, um, doing research for a story I'm, um, writing."

Gretta relaxes. Her brown eyes become marshmallow soft. "Of course they love me. Didn't you listen to what I said the other day? Having a baby is the easy part. It's the bringing up that's to do with love."

I begin to feel better. Then I remember. "Gretta, what if your birth parents suddenly turned up? How do you reckon you'd feel?"

"That'd be a shock," says Gretta.

"And what if your parents, the ones who'd been caring for you, hadn't told you that you were adopted? What would you do?"

"That would be a huge shock," says Gretta. "I've always known about being adopted. I reckon if I didn't know and my birth parents fronted up, I'd faint. They'd have to call an ambulance and take me to hospital. I'd wake up there, take one look at my birth parents, and faint again. I'd keep fainting and fainting. Then I'd get a stomach-ache. I always get that when I'm nervous. I'd faint and then the stomach-ache would wake me up. Then I'd ..."

"OK, Gretta, I get the point."

Gretta suddenly sees Mandy and runs off.

I feel awful. I study my hands. My thumbs are very long. One night Mum and Dad remarked on how long they were and how *they* didn't have long thumbs. Perhaps they'd tried to tell me in the past. Maybe they were waiting for me to ask them about myself. After all, Dad mentioned he didn't get dandruff. His feet didn't smell. They both had short thumbs. They'd been careful to tell me that.

I remember Mum saying how easy it was to toilet-train me. Not like Bub Tub, who may be the only kid to go to school in nappies if she doesn't shape up.

Maybe I really come from a long line of easily toilet-trained children.

I don't talk much at dinner and I don't even eat much. I stare helplessly from Mum to Dad. How can I ever begin to thank them for taking care of me all this time?

I look at Bub Tub. So she's not my flesh-and-blood sister. She's got Mum's eyes and Dad's smile and that's it. I'd always been glad that she didn't resemble me. Now I'd give away my Lance Spear comic collection just to find out we'd inherited the same freckles.

Later Dad smears ointment on Bub Tub while Mum and I clear away the dishes. Mum says to me, "Um, Danny, there's something I need to talk about with you."

She seems suddenly nervous, or is it just my imagination? Is she biting her lower lip or is she just trying to get rid of that bit of potato stuck there?

"Sit down, Danny," says Mum. "We'll finish off the washing-up later."

Mum smoothes her jeans and tries to look relaxed, but I can tell. It's that other woman. The one who is my birth mother. She wants me back. She and my birth father. They've been hanging around outside the school grounds trying to get a glimpse of me. My birth mother is frantic. She needs a skin graft to her elbow because she's got dreadful boils there and only someone related to her, like say a son, can help.

I sit awkwardly on the kitchen chair. Somewhere in the house I can hear Dad singing "Incey, wincey spider" to Bub Tub.

"It's like this," says Mum. "You remember Aunty Freda?"

"Huh? Dad's youngest sister? Sure."

I hold my breath. So she's the one. I've heard that it happens. The family of the baby don't want it adopted out so someone, perhaps an aunt and uncle, decide to take the baby in. Aunty Freda? I can't remember the shape of her thumbs, but her hair is definitely reddish-brown.

"Danny," says Mum. "You've got that look in your eyes you get when you're daydreaming. Listen to me."

She is leaning across the kitchen table, frowning. She has no right to frown at me. I'm the one who should be frowning.

She puts her hand over mine. "Well, Danny, Aunty Freda's splitting up with her boyfriend. She's in a bad way and she needs a break. I've invited her to stay here for a week or so. Now, I know how you'll hate sharing Bubby's room but there's no way around it. I was going to wait before telling you because you've been carrying on about her spots, but I really don't think they're contagious.

"It's only for a week. If the smell in Bub Tub's room is too bad you can sleep on the sofa."

I feel my eyes bursting out of their sockets. My head feels as if it's about to explode.

92

"You mean I'm not adopted?"

"Danny," says Mum, and she takes her hand away and moves back in surprise. "Whatever gave you that idea? What are you talking about? Are you sickening for something? Haven't you heard a word that I've said?"

"You said I'd have to move in with Bub Tub when Aunty Freda stays with us."

Mum shakes her head. "You're definitely coming down with something. I expected you to make a scene."

"This is very cool," I tell Mum.

That weekend Aunty Freda, who is as miserable as a fish at the end of a hook, moves in. She is biting her nails and has nasty things to say about her ex-boyfriend.

I move in with Bub Tub. She is very pleased about this.

"Ayo Anny. Da doody abbid phlo."

It is very difficult to share a bedroom with Bub Tub. She talks to herself non-stop, rattles her mobile, and stands up in her cot and screams. All this is in addition to the smell, which is terrible.

Bub Tub is very attached to the daggy parrot. She keeps pushing it in my hands and saying, "Ook, Danny. Itty cocky."

I notice that after I touch the parrot I start to itch. And itch and itch.

I'm suddenly covered with spots and look extremely off.

Mum takes Bub Tub and me to the doctor.

"It's the stuffed parrot," she tells Dad triumphantly when we return. "I should have thought about it earlier. Both kids are allergic to its feathers."

Dad is sad. "OK, I know when I'm beaten. I'll keep Polly on a high shelf at the shop."

"Allergies sometimes run in families," Mum tells me. "Your grandmother was a very allergic person, and sometimes I break out in hives. I guess you get it from my side of the family."

I start to laugh.

"Hey," says Mum. "What's so funny?"

I try to explain. "It's just that I thought you were my aunt and my aunt was my mum and my real dad had dandruff and stinky feet."

Mum shakes her head. "Danny, I think those spots have settled in your brain."

She's probably right.

other ove

One Saturday morning I am helping Dad in the deli.

Mandy Miller comes into the shop. She waves to me. I feel awkward. It's a bit embarrassing to be caught stacking rolls of toilet paper.

"Hi, Danny." She smiles at me. "I've come to buy some pet food for Sookie."

Sookie is Mandy's Silky Terrier. Mandy has had her for about eight months. I point out to Mandy where the pet food cans stand in neat little lines on a bottom shelf near where I'm working.

She bends and picks up two cans. "You'll never guess what," she says. "Sookie's pregnant."

I begin to unload cans of tinned peaches.

"Hey, that's very cool. You're going to have all these puppies running around."

"I know. Though we can't understand how she got pregnant. We keep her inside most of the time."

"Yeah?" This conversation is getting vaguely embarrassing. "When are the puppies, um, due?"

"We're not sure. We're going to take her to the vet today."

Mandy holds up two cans of Bob's Pet Food. "I'll take these to your dad at the counter. Are you doing anything when you finish here? Mum's baking chocolate cookies. You could drop in on your way home."

Mandy's mum's chocolate cookies are fantastic. Out of this world.

"Um, maybe," I say. I've been to Mandy's house before, but only with a few friends from school. I've never been by myself. I hesitate. Then I remember her mum's chocolate cookies. "I reckon I can."

After I've finished helping Dad I go to Mandy's house and knock on the door. Her mum opens it. "Ah, Danny, isn't it?" she says brightly. She is a tall lady with hair pushed back from her face and clear blue eyes like Mandy's.

I follow her to the kitchen where Mandy is sitting at the table. There is a big plate of very good-smelling cookies in front of her, and she is stuffing her face.

"Sit down," she says through a chocolate moustache. "Eat." So I sit next to Mandy and stuff my face too. The cookies are great.

"Don't eat too many," says Mandy's mum. "You'll get sick."

Sick? Is she kidding?

Mandy's dog, Sookie, trots into the room. She's a tiny, fluffy thing with long silver fur, mournful eyes and practically no tail. She's fat. I guess that's because she's having puppies.

"Don't give any cookies to Sookie," says Mandy. "She's putting on a lot of weight. I'm so excited about the puppies, though I still don't know how she could have got pregnant."

I worry about this remark. Maybe I should lend Mandy one of those books about how babies come into the world.

"When are you taking her to the vet?" I splutter as I put two cookies in my mouth at once.

"Soon. We want to get her checked out. Though we're quite sure she's having puppies."

"How do you know? Maybe she's just fat."

"No," says Mandy firmly. "She's definitely pregnant. You should see the way she's carrying on. She runs around the house, hiding in cupboards. Dogs do that, you know, when they're pregnant. They go nuts looking for a warm place to have their puppies.

And what about her tummy? Also, her nipples are beginning to swell. That's because they're filling up with milk."

I really wish Mandy hadn't said this. It's put me right off my chocolate cookies. Nipples filling up with milk—it's the kind of thing I'd rather not hear about until I'm much older.

Mandy hops off her chair and goes over to Sookie. She bends down and pats her. Sookie is kind of cute. Those little pointed ears and that long, licky tongue. She woof woofs around Mandy. Mandy picks her up.

"You little Sookieums," she says. "You dear little Sook Sook." This is pretty gross talk and if it wasn't Mandy Miller carrying on I might throw up.

Her mum walks into the kitchen. "It's time to go to the vet's. Mandy, you sit in the back seat and hold on to Sookie. You know what she's like in the car. Danny, tell me where you live, and we can drop you off."

So I follow Mrs Miller and Mandy out of the house. We get into the back of Mrs Miller's little green car and Mandy holds Sookie on her knee and strokes her. She says things like, "You dear little pregnant Sook Sook." Apart from Mrs Miller's fantastic chocolate cookies and the way the sunlight makes Mandy's hair shiny, this is turning into a very off experience.

Sookie suddenly begins to shake.

"She doesn't like going for a drive," says Mandy to

me as her mother backs the car out of the driveway. "It upsets her stomach. It makes her throw up."

I move right away from Mandy when she says that. She whispers encouraging words to Sookie, like, "Think about other things, Sookie. Don't think about the way the car is bumping around."

Sookie continues to shake. I see her stomach heaving. I don't know whether it is the puppies jumping around inside her or if she is gearing herself to puke. I am dead relieved when Mrs Miller stops her car at the corner of my street.

I jump out as quickly as I can, say goodbye and walk home.

Later that day Mum gives me some letters to post. On the way to the post box I see Mandy walking Sookie. Sookie trots along beside her and wags her tiny tail.

"Hi, Danny," says Mandy. "You won't believe what the vet said about Sookie."

I kneel and pat Sookie on her silky fur. She lifts up her head and gives me a sloppy lick on my hand.

"There aren't any puppies," says Mandy.

This is very surprising. Mandy is looking sad.

"We were so sure. The vet said that Sookie is having a phantom pregnancy."

"Huh? What's that?"

"Sookie just *thinks* she's pregnant. She's never had

99

puppies and the vet reckons she'd really like to and that she's talked herself into thinking she's pregnant."

"That sounds weird."

I imagine Sookie having a chat to herself. "See here, Sookie. You really are pregnant." "No, I'm not. I just think I am." "Can't you hear what I'm saying? You *are*."

"It *is* weird," says Mandy.

"But what about her, um, nip …" I can't bring myself to say the word.

"You mean her nipples," says Mandy loudly. I look quickly around. Fortunately there is no one walking by who has heard Mandy say that word. "Well, it can happen with a phantom pregnancy. She's talked herself into believing she's having puppies and her body's begun to change."

"But her stomach's so fat."

"The vet says he thinks it's just air."

"Air?" I say. "That's very off, Mandy. When will Sookie discover that she's not going to be a mum and is just carrying a big bag of air?"

"We don't know," says Mandy. "I guess that's up to Sookie. But meantime, the vet said to be as kind to her as possible and to give her a lot of attention."

Sookie definitely doesn't strike me as deprived. Her silver coat is almost as shiny as Mandy's hair. Her eyes are bright and her nose is moist.

"Poor Sookie," says Mandy. "It's really sad. She wants puppies so much. I reckon we should let her get pregnant when she comes into season. Do you know what that means?"

I watch a red car passing by. Of course I know what "coming into season" means. It's a time when animals can get pregnant. They have a special scent which attracts animals of the opposite sex. Yuk. I may throw up if Mandy doesn't stop all this personal talk.

"I'd better post these letters," I say quickly. "Otherwise the plane may take off without them." I try to laugh.

"I'll walk with you," says Mandy. Then she says, "Anyway, Mum wants to get Sookie de-sexed. Do you know what that means?"

If Mandy doesn't stop talking like this I'll go off my brain.

Luckily she doesn't wait for a reply. "It's a real shame, but Mum says if Sookie isn't pregnant now, she should be de-sexed. It's the responsible thing to do."

"She's right. Otherwise you'll have four little Bub Tubs running around the house without nappies. That'll be gross."

Mandy frowns at me. "I don't think it'll be gross. I think it would be great. I'd look after them. And then my little Sookie would feel better about herself."

"But you'd have to give the puppies away eventually, Mandy," I say. "And then Sookie would be in a really bad way."

Mandy bites her lip. "Yes, I guess you're right. Either way Sookie has a big problem."

She reaches down and picks Sookie up. Sookie's stomach is really big. Full of air, the vet said. Wow!

Time goes by. Sookie's stomach continues to grow. Mandy continues to worry about her. Sookie continues to run around the house searching for a place to have her puppies.

One day when school has finished, Corky and I are making our way across the school yard to the gate. Suddenly Corky stops walking. He turns his head to one side.

"Did you hear that?"

"What?" I say. I can hear the cicadas buzzing away, the kids rushing home, cars honking. There's plenty to hear.

"It's like a tiny squeak," says Corky. "Yeah, there it goes again."

I listen. Corky is right. A high-pitched little squeak is coming from … there.

Corky drops his school bag and runs to where a little furry thing is scampering around.

"Hey, it's a kitten."

A little black-and-white ball of fluff is running around chasing its tail.

Corky grabs the kitten. It curls up in his arms, stares at him with big luminous eyes and says "Meow," which in cat talk, as everyone knows, means "G'day. Nice to meet you."

"It must be lost or dumped," says Corky.

The kitten is a bit thin. Its eyes are bright, though, and it's very affectionate. It purrs like the tick-tock of a clock.

"What do we do with it?" I reach over and rub the kitten's stomach.

"Well, we can't leave it here," says Corky. "I'll just have to take it home."

He opens the top buttons of his shirt and puts the kitten inside. It curls up with just its little pointed face and two paws peeking out.

"Now what were we talking about before this kitten turned up?" says Corky. "Oh yes, my stamp collection. Bring over all your swaps this weekend. And your comic swaps too."

"Meow," agrees the kitten and she chews a button on Corky's shirt.

The following day is Saturday. I go around to Corky's house with my stamp and comic swaps.

"How's the kitten?" I ask.

"You mean Itsy? She's fine, but I can't keep her. Mum says she's giving her hay fever. I've got to take her to the vet's soon. He's going to put a sign in his window to see if anyone owns her. If no one does he said he'll try to find a home for her."

Corky and I sprawl out on the carpet in his bedroom. Itsy comes dashing in. She's very active. She runs around with a small ball of string and is soon tangled up in it. She also manages to do a poo on one of my Lance Spear comics.

Corky's mother comes into the room. She sniffs the air, then sees the poo on the comic.

"Get that kitten out of here, Corky. And when Danny leaves, take her to the vet's. I don't want her here any longer. Clear up her mess. Thank goodness she did it on the comic and not on the carpet."

I want to tell Corky's mum that to do a poo on Lance Spear is very uncool and I would feel better if Itsy had done it on the carpet, but she probably wouldn't understand. Corky holds his nose and takes the comic out of the room. This is very sad. I now have one less comic to swap.

When it's time for me to leave, Corky puts Itsy in a small shoe box with an old sock.

"I feel rotten taking her to the vet's," he tells me. "Because if no one claims her and he can't find her a home, I reckon he'll put her down."

That makes me feel rotten too.

We leave Corky's house and walk to the vet's. His lawn smells, but I guess that is because all of his patients do a big pee before coming in to the surgery.

Itsy peeks at the receptionist with her big bright eyes. The receptionist takes the shoe box from Corky. We both say goodbye to Itsy. She meows back at us. Corky shakes his head.

"This is the worst thing I've ever had to do."

After we leave the vet's, I offer Corky some bubblegum but he says he doesn't want any, which shows how bad he's feeling.

The next day Corky phones me.

"I called the vet's. They've got a sign up in the window and they've checked with the animal shelter, but no one's come to claim Itsy. They reckon she just got dumped. What a lousy thing to do. They're going to wait a week, then they'll put her down. I feel terrible."

So do I. I ask Mum and Dad if we can keep Itsy, but they are firm. "No, Danny, and that's that."

On Monday Mandy says to me at school, "Sookie isn't looking pregnant any more."

"Really? What happened to her huge stomach?"

Mandy's face is red. She turns away.

"Well, yesterday I was with her when she suddenly rolled over on her back. She made a kind of whining sound. And then she well, um, well, she passed a lot of wind. It went on for ages. But by the time she'd finished, her stomach was a lot flatter and she seemed more comfortable."

"What? You mean she gave birth to a …"

"Don't say the word, Danny. Yes, that's what happened."

I start to laugh. "You've got a crazy dog. Is she still running around looking for places to have puppies?"

"No. She's sad though and she whimpers all the time. I guess she really thought she was going to have puppies. Giving birth to wind must be disappointing."

I crack up.

Days roll by. Corky phones the vet's to check if anyone has claimed Itsy. No one has. "I reckon Itsy has about three days left to live on Planet Earth," he tells me.

Then, out of the blue, Mandy phones me on Saturday.

"You should see Sookie. She's so frisky and happy—and guess what?"

"What?"

"She's had a baby."

"Huh—but I thought you said …? Hey, the vet was wrong after all. She really was pregnant then."

"Come on over," says Mandy. "And ask Corky to come too. Mum's baked some more of her chocolate cookies."

So I phone Corky, who isn't the least bit interested in going to Mandy's house, but is very keen to eat her mum's chocolate cookies.

"They're awesome. I remember when Mandy brought some to school. I don't want to see Mandy and her crazy dog. Mandy's OK, but the way she carries on and on about Sookie is nuts. Honestly, I'd never go on like that about a pet. I liked Itsy, but I reckon I'm over her now. She's in cat heaven I guess.

"Anyway," continues Corky, "even if Mandy talks weird around Sookie, I'll come just to eat her mum's cookies."

I get off the phone, quickly tell Mum I'm off to Mandy's for a while and dart down the road. I slow down as I approach Mandy's place. I don't want her to think I've rushed over, and I don't want Corky to catch me out of breath.

Mrs Miller opens the front door. She has a patch of flour on her nose. "Mandy's in the back garden, Danny." Then she looks past me. "Hi, um, Corky, isn't it?"

Corky strolls up the footpath. He stares at Mrs Miller expectantly.

"They're in the kitchen, Corky. Help yourself."

We walk into the kitchen and stuff Mrs Miller's delicious cookies in our mouths. Corky puts two in his pocket for later. We go through the back sunroom to the garden.

Mandy is sitting on the lawn. She's chewing a blade of grass and thoughtfully watching ...

"Hey," says Corky. "Isn't that ..."

Sookie is walking around the yard. In her mouth, being carried by the scruff of her neck, is ... Itsy!

Mandy sees us. Her smile is the size of Bondi Beach.

"We got her from the vet's. Sookie thinks the kitten's her new baby. The kitten thinks she's found her mother."

Sookie gently lowers Itsy to the grass. The kitten lies on her fluffy tummy and allows herself to be thoroughly licked. Sookie's tail wags like crazy as the kitten smiles a kitten smile at her.

Corky drops down beside Itsy. He ruffles her fur.

"It's great, isn't it?" says Mandy.

"It's even better than when Helen the Horrible got laryngitis," says Corky.

Mandy and Corky sit on the grass next to Itsy and Sookie. I stand near the back fence, watching.

"My Sookie is so cute," Mandy says. "You should see her when she's curled up sleeping with the kitten."

"Yeah?" says Corky, his eyes bright. "That sounds cool. Hey, Itsy, it's me. Your old dad. How about a sandpaper lick?"

Then the impossible happens. Corky reaches into his pockets and pulls out Mrs Miller's cookies. He'd normally die for them. He breaks them into small pieces and gives them to Sookie and Itsy.

There is serious family stuff going on here. I fish around in my own pockets, check on my bubblegum supply, give Corky and Mandy a wave and head for home.

So you're Mr and Mrs Thompson

I have no idea who these people are standing around me. Two of them have friendly, familiar faces, but I just can't remember their names.

The other one is dressed in white and looks like a doctor. He leans over the bed and shines something bright in my eyes.

Bed. I'm in a hospital bed. The walls are white, the ceiling is white and my sheet is white.

This must be a dream. Any moment now I'm going to wake up in my own bedroom at home ... hey— where *is* home? And who am I? What's my name?

I start to feel dizzy. I've can't remember a thing. It must be because of this awful headache I have.

"Well, young man," says the doctor. "We're glad you're awake. You've given your parents quite a shock."

This man and woman come charging at me like a bull charging a matador. They hug me and the lady has tears in her eyes. I feel sad when I see the tears, though I'm not sure why.

"Who are you?" I ask the lady, because she's awfully familiar and I can almost remember who she is.

"What?" asks the lady, and she stops slobbering over me.

"Danny, don't you know who I am?"

"No," I say politely.

The lady turns and says to the doctor, "Do something. He's lost his memory."

"Hmm," says the doctor. "He's had a bad concussion, but we've done a scan. I'm sure this is just a temporary setback."

The man who is with the lady starts to slobber over me now. He kisses my cheek and strokes my hair.

"Danny, hey, it's us. Mum and Dad."

"You seem familiar," I say puzzled. "Are you sure you're my parents? You're not neighbours or school teachers?"

"Your name is Danny Thompson." The doctor takes out his pen from a pocket and writes something in a notebook. Then he looks at me. "These are your parents. Don't worry too much about remembering things right now. It will all come back."

"So you're Mr and Mrs Thompson," I say politely to the couple, who seem very distressed.

Mrs Thompson puts a hand to her mouth. She starts to cry. Mr Thompson stands there, his eyes frightened. I seem to have said the wrong thing.

The doctor says, "Let him rest now. After all, it was a nasty accident."

"I'm going to stay right here," Mrs Thompson says in a familiar, stubborn voice. She sits down beside my bed. I feel good about this, though I don't know why. "Roger, you go home. Bub Tub is at Mrs Cohen's place. I'll phone you later."

Bub Tub. That's a very familiar name. Why is my nose wrinkling up? And why am I suddenly sniffing the air around me?

Mr Thompson walks out of the room with the doctor. Mrs Thompson pats my cheek.

"You had an awful accident, dear. Just rest."

"What happened?" I ask.

"You were at the park with Corky and Taffy. Corky told me that you were standing on top of the monkey bars saying you were Lance Spear. You somehow lost your balance. It was a bad fall, and you hit your head. We had to rush you to hospital. You've been out to it for two days."

"You mean I've been unconscious?"

"Yes, dear. But you're OK. Now just rest."

"Thanks, Mrs Thompson," I say. The lady doesn't seem too pleased with that. I'm just being polite. She frowns and more tears fill her eyes. I want to say something else to her but I'm tired. My eyes feel heavy and just won't stay open.

When I wake up later my head feels a bit better. Mrs Thompson is still sitting beside the bed. She smiles at me.

"Feeling better, Danny?"

"Yes, thanks, Mrs Thompson."

She bites her lip. "Can't you remember anything, Danny?"

I start to think. "Not really. I can remember the name Lance Spear. You mentioned it before. Is he in a comic?"

Mrs Thompson looks pleased. "Very good. He's the hero in your favourite comic. It's a start. But what about me? Don't you remember anything about your dad and me?"

Small bits of memory unclog. "Salami. That word just popped into my head."

Mrs Thompson's voice is excited. "Wonderful.

That's what your dad sells at his shop."

"He has a salami shop?"

"Not just salami. He sells everything there. Your memory's starting to come back."

"I'm getting tired," I say because all this thinking has made me dizzy. "I think I'll just go back to sleep now, Mrs Thompson."

I sleep and wake up. Then I fall asleep again. This seems to go on for a few days. Whenever I wake up Mr or Mrs Thompson is sitting by the bed. Sometimes a doctor comes and shines a light in my eyes and says something.

Slowly I start to feel better. My head clears and I begin to tolerate the gross hospital mush I am now given. Mr Thompson brings me Lance Spear comics to read.

I still can't remember much at all though. Knowing that Mr Thompson sells salami and that I like Lance Spear comics is not a lot of memory to carry around.

"Your friends are going to come and visit you, Danny," says Mrs Thompson as she plumps my pillow.

"Friends," I say. "Hey, that's cool. I've got friends."

Mrs Thompson gets tears in her eyes again and I wish I knew what was the right thing to say.

That afternoon two boys and a girl come into my room. They all seem familiar.

"I'd have brought you some bubblegum," says one of the boys. He has straight brown hair and a curly grin. "But your dad said you're not allowed junk food. How can he call bubblegum junk?"

This boy gives me some more Lance Spear comics to read.

"Thanks," I say to him. "You're very kind."

"Huh?" he says. "Kind. That's a weird thing to say."

The girl standing beside him pokes him in the back. "Be quiet, Corky. He still doesn't know who you are. Poor Danny."

I look at the girl and suddenly feel hot and cold. That's strange. I notice that light coming through the window makes her hair very shiny.

"I brought you some fruit." She puts a brown paper bag on the small table beside my bed. "Hope you get better soon, Danny."

"Thanks," I say.

Then a bigger boy, who is a bit plump and is shifting around uncomfortably from foot to foot, says, "Hi, Danny. Do you know who I am?"

"No, but the word 'ear' suddenly popped into my head. Does that mean anything?"

The three of them start laughing.

"He's getting better already," says the boy who

gave me the Lance Spear comics.

Mrs Thompson, who has been standing near the window, watching us, says, "Just stay a few minutes. I don't want him to get too tired."

So my three new friends stay for a short while. It's fun. They give me this huge, daggy Get Well card from Year 6 at my school. Year 6. My school. I try to remember.

"Steaming glasses. Those words just came to me."

They crack up at that. "Mr King's glasses," says the boy called Taffy.

Later, when they've gone, Mrs Thompson comes over to the bed. "Well, how did you feel seeing them, Danny? Did it bring back any memories?"

"Almost," I say. "It's like my memories are trapped in a room and occasionally a few words that don't make sense just leak out from under the door."

"Well, the doctor says you're getting on fine. He says you'll be able to come home in a few days. All the tests show you're OK. The concussion has affected your memory right now, but in time it will come back."

Still, I feel worried. What if I go home and my memory doesn't come back? What if I lose my friends because I can't remember their names? What if I can't even find my way to the corner shop because I don't know where the corner is?

I lie in bed, staring at the white walls and the white ceiling. I try desperately to remember my home. The only thing I recall is a white fridge with a tub of vanilla ice-cream in it.

"Dad's bringing your sister, Penny, to see you soon," says Mrs Thompson. "You've always called her Bub Tub. Does the name ring a bell?"

Bub Tub. I can almost place it.

"What does she look like?" I ask.

Mrs Thompson begins to cry again. I notice that there are dark smudges under her eyes and remember that either she or Mr Thompson has been sitting by my bed since I first woke up in hospital.

"I'm sorry," I say. "I'm trying to remember."

Mrs Thompson leans across the bed and strokes my forehead. "It will come back. Sooner or later something will happen to open that door where your memories are, Danny."

Mr Thompson walks in. This little kid toddles alongside him. She's dressed in a pink dress and has a bib around her neck.

"Ayo, Anny." She comes running towards me. Mrs Thompson lifts her up and puts her beside me on the bed.

I stare into the kid's blue eyes. I notice that dribble is dripping down her chin.

"Hi, um, Bub Tub," I say politely.

Then I find myself sniffing the air. I don't know why I'm doing this but I can't help myself. There's this off smell around this little kid. It's like a cloud that is attached to her.

How can I tell Mr and Mrs Thompson that their daughter pongs?

The smell? It's so familiar.

Suddenly there is this stretched feeling in my brain. Like hinges on boxes are pulling free. Like doors are opening. Like Lance Spear has suddenly reached the top of a huge alien mountain.

"Get her away from me, Mum. She stinks!"

"Mum, you called me Mum," squeals Mum.

"And who am I?" asks Dad excitedly.

"Dad the salami king. That's who. It's all coming back. I'm Danny Thompson. You're my parents and she's my sister. I'll tell you anything you want to know, just get her away from me."

Dad gathers Bub Tub in his arms.

"You're OK," says Mum and she gives me yet another sloppy kiss.

Then she turns to Dad. "You're definitely a genius, Roger. A regular Einstein."

"What are you talking about?" I ask.

Dad winks at me. "I told your mother that bringing Bub Tub to see you with a full nappy would do the trick."

Bub Tub looks from one face to the other. "Anny, ooble phlub da doody, iggle bug." I can't quite remember what that means.